Olsen pointed at the empty leather sheath in the glove compartment. "What is that?"

"My grandfather gave me a knife, a Buck knife for Christmas. But—"

"Did you take it out?"

His throat constricted. "I don't think so. No, I didn't."

"When was the last time you saw it?"

"Maybe a week ago. I checked the air pressure on my tires when I filled up with gas."

He stared at the empty sheath, and his eyes glazed over as he thought about the dream he'd had while he lay unconscious on the football field. At the end of it, Myra had appeared amid the chaos in the kiva and a knife slashed at her throat.

Rob MacGregor is the author of *Prophecy Rock*, which won the 1996 Mystery Writers of America Edgar Award for young adult fiction, and ten other novels. He resides in South Florida and travels frequently to the Southwest.

ALSO AVAILABLE IN LAUREL-LEAF BOOKS:

Hawk Moon

ROB MACGREGOR

LAUREL-LEAF
BOOKS

Published by
Bantam Doubleday Dell Books for Young Readers
a division of
Bantam Doubleday Dell Publishing Group, Inc.
1540 Broadway
New York, New York 10036

Visit us on the Web! www.bdd.com

Educators and librarians, visit the BDD Teacher's Resource Center at www.bdd.com/teachers

ISBN: 0-440-22741-0

RL: 5.8

Reprinted by arrangement with Simon & Schuster Books for Young Readers

Printed in the United States of America

August 1998

10 9 8 7 6 5 4 3 2 1

To Trish

PROLOGUE

The ghost town seemed to shimmer like a mirage in the moonlight. It spooked her. This place had always spooked her. Even at midday.

As they walked into the town, a dust devil swirled down the street. The wind moaned through the old buildings. Myra wondered what it would have been like to live here in the old days, maybe as the daughter of a prospector and his wife who'd crossed the Great Plains in a wagon train.

Ashcroft came into being in the summer of 1880, near the road leading over Taylor Pass. Within a year, about five hundred people lived in Ashcroft, about the same as Aspen at that time. Soon, a telegraph wire crossed the pass connecting the two towns, and the population swelled to two thousand. But the good times didn't last long. By the end of the century, a depressed mood swept through the mining communities as the value of silver fell, and Ashcroft was abandoned. Now, more than a hundred years later, what remained of the town was slowly collapsing.

Myra glanced at her companion, then quickened her pace through the chilly autumn night. She stopped in front of one of the buildings in the heart of Ashcroft and peered through the entry. The door had disappeared long ago; the interior was a dark hole. A whisper of wind seemed to beckon her. She felt her heart pounding.

"You wanna go inside?" Will asked.

She turned to Will Lansa, whose brown eyes stared intently at her. In the light of the full moon, his high cheekbones emphasized his Native American heritage. "I don't know. It gives me the creeps."

"It's just an old building, Myra." He stepped through the doorway, and she lost sight of him.

"Will?"

"Hey, come and take a look at this, will ya?"

"What is it?"

"Come here. Hurry."

She hesitated, then moved into the building. She smelled the odor of damp, rotting wood. But there was something more here, too. Something that made her feel tense and cold. The beams creaked and moaned. Even in here, the cool wind penetrated her bones.

"Will?"

"Over here."

She took two cautious steps in the direction of his voice, wishing she hadn't followed him. Then she saw him standing in front of a window bathed in faint moonlight.

"It's a red fox," he whispered.

She relaxed her shoulders, exhaling, then took another step. "A fox? What's it—"

Something tugged on her scarf. Tugged again. She shrieked, clawed the scarf off, and bolted for the door. She raced into the middle of the wide dirt road, and for a moment she thought she saw herself from high above as she spun in circles at the very center of the ghost town.

"Jeez, Myra. What happened?" Will asked as he loped out to her.

"Something grabbed me. It pulled my scarf."

"Myra, you probably hooked your scarf on a nail or something. I'll go get it."

She reached for his arm. "No. I want to get out of here right now."

"What about your scarf?"

"I don't care. It's old."

They walked in silence past several dark buildings. When they were out of the town and on the path leading to the parking lot, Myra starting feeling more at ease. "I guess that was sort of silly of me to get afraid like that."

"I can see how it might happen."

"Do the Hopis believe in ghosts?" She knew that Will's knowledge of Hopi ways was limited, that until this past summer, when he'd visited his father, he'd known very little about his heritage.

"We believe in our ancestors, the power of the kachinas, and the reality of the spirit world. I don't know about ghosts."

It was the first time she'd heard him speak of himself as a Hopi. His experience with his father, who was chief of police on the Hopi reservation, had made a strong impact.

Even though they'd started seeing each other again this fall, Myra had noticed a difference in Will. He was quieter, more introspective. It was as if he were always mulling over things that had happened during the summer. From what he'd told her, there was plenty to think about.

But Will wasn't the only one who had undergone some trying times. She'd asked him to meet her here because she had something to tell him and she wanted to do it away from school and friends.

They reached the parking lot, and Will walked her to her mother's minivan. She turned to face him, and the brisk wind rippled through her hair. Events of the summer had left her confused and frightened. She'd remained silent about what she'd seen and found out, but the others involved were watching her too closely. She was certain something was going to happen, and before it did she wanted to tell Will about it.

Will didn't touch her, didn't try to kiss her. He just stared at her, his chiseled features not giving her any hint of what he was thinking.

Talking to him lately had been nearly impossible. He was busy with football practice every afternoon after school, and this week the coach had extended the practice time an hour in preparation for the final game of the season against Leadville for the conference title. Today, though, he'd agreed to meet her, and now she was going to tell him everything. She hoped he could help her decide what she should do.

Then they both spoke at the same time. "Will."

"Myra."

They laughed nervously.

"There's something I've got to tell you," he said. "Something important."

"Me too, but go ahead. You first."

"I don't feel right about seeing you anymore." He shrugged. "It's just not working out for me."

Myra was caught off guard. She knew their relationship had been strained lately, but she hadn't been expecting that. "Why not? Did I do something?"

"No, it's got nothing to do with you. I've got to be alone now. I need to figure some things out."

"Does that mean we can't talk to each other anymore?"

"I hope we can still be friends, but . . ."

"Yeah, I know how it is." She turned her back on him and opened the minivan door. "I guess we won't be going to Paige's tomorrow night."

"Let's talk tomorrow at lunch," he said.

"Forget it!"

If he wanted to break up, that was it. She slammed the door. Will stared at her through the window, then walked off toward his Jeep. She heard the engine rev up as she reached into her jacket for her keys.

He hadn't even asked what she'd been planning to tell him. He was so caught up in his own world—his football and his musings about his Hopi self—he didn't even know there was something wrong in her life and it involved people he knew. Now Myra was at a loss as to who she should turn to, what she should say. But she just couldn't hold it back any longer. She hated to involve her mother, but . . .

"Hi, Myra."

She jumped in her seat, spun around. "My God, you scared me. What are you doing in here? How did you get here?"

She saw a blur of movement and something heavy slammed against her head. She groaned at the terrible pain that exploded in her head. She reached for the door handle, struggling to escape, but then she was struck again. Her hand fell away and she sank into a vast sea far below the waves of pain.

ONE

As he went through the lunch line, almost everyone had an encouraging word for Will, and he couldn't help enjoying his fame. All week long, kids he didn't even know had greeted him in the hall and wished him luck in the big game.

Not only was the conference championship at stake but also Will needed to gain only sixty-two more yards and he would be in the school's record books. Since he'd been averaging over 150 yards a game, he was sure today would be his day.

He looked for Myra as he carried his tray into the lunchroom, expecting to see her at the table where she and her friends from the art crowd usually sat. He wondered if she would act as if he didn't exist or, worse, act as if he was just another student, as if nothing had ever happened between them. Whatever, he knew it was going to be awkward. But she wasn't at the table or anywhere else in the lunchroom.

"Lansa, get over here," a familiar voice called out. Claude Kirkpatrick, the star tackle, waved at him.

At six foot four and 225 pounds with curly red hair and freckles, Kirkpatrick was hard to miss. "We're planning our victory celebration."

"Don't you think it's a little early for that?" he said, sitting down between Kirkpatrick and Aaron Thomas, the quarterback.

"Coach would call it positive reinforcement," Thomas said, running his hand through his thick, blond hair, which was parted in the middle and cut short on the sides. He had steely, blue eyes, a square jaw and, by most accounts, was the most popular kid in school, especially with the girls.

"So when are you going to break the rushing record, the first quarter or are you going to make us wait until the second?" Kirkpatrick asked, slapping Will on the shoulder.

"Hey, I'll be happy just to make the record."

"Oh, listen to Mr. Modest," Paige Davis said as she stopped behind Will, resting a hand lightly on his back. She was tall and slender and had the looks and grace of a fashion model, the kind who appeared on the covers of magazines.

Paige and Aaron were both children of celebrities. Her mother was a movie star and her father a producer, while both of Aaron's parents were actors. Claude's father, Bower Kirkpatrick, was Pitkin County sheriff, and his name and face seemed to be everywhere since he'd launched his campaign for a third term.

Will's father, Pete Lansa, also worked in law

enforcement, but his territory—the Hopi reservation—was a world away from Aspen. He had promised to come here for the big game, and Will hoped he'd make it.

"Have you seen Myra?"

Paige shook her blond hair off her shoulder. "Not today. She probably skipped lunch to work on her sculpture. She's such an *ar-teest*, you know." Paige was joking, but Will thought he heard a hint of jealousy in her voice.

Myra was from a well-to-do family that had been involved in banking and politics for decades in Aspen. Like a lot of longtime residents, her parents had mixed feelings about the influence of Hollywood stars on Aspen. But Myra got along with everyone and was one of the best liked students in the school.

Paige bent over and whispered something in Claude's ear, then kissed him on the cheek and rubbed his curly hair. They'd been nearly inseparable since the first day of school this fall. Claude managed to see Paige almost every day after football practice, which meant that he wasn't doing much homework, if any.

Will thought about Myra again. Everything had just gotten too complicated, and he felt he'd been ignoring her. But now he wondered if he'd made a mistake last night. When Will and Claude were the only ones left at the table, he told Claude what had happened.

"I'm not surprised. Things really haven't been the same with you two since you came back. I bet that

Hopi girl from the summer is still on your mind."

Will had told Claude about Ellie Polongahoya and the strange incident involving the Hopi prophecies, but he hadn't said anything about the pilgrimage he'd taken with his father or the visions he'd had of the powerful being known as Masau.

He shrugged. "It's not that. It just seems like Myra and I can't talk to each other anymore. I have a hard time telling her about the things on my mind, and, I guess the truth is, I haven't taken the time to listen to her."

"That happens, Will. But don't let it get to you, not today. Hey, look at the time. We better get down to the locker room." They were done with classes for the day, but they had a team meeting before they dressed for the game.

"You've got to stay focused. That's what's important," Claude said for the third time as they headed for the locker room. It was almost as if he were telling himself as well as Will. "You can make it all in the first quarter, but if you don't, don't worry about it. Keep your focus."

It wasn't like Claude to harp on a point, but Will figured that his breakup with Myra had gotten Claude thinking about his own future with Paige.

Just as they reached the stairway leading down to the locker room, Will caught sight of Myra's mother as she entered the administrative offices. Maybe Myra was sick and Mrs. Hodges was picking something up for her. He considered going over and saying something to her, but Claude called to him from the doorway of the locker room.

"Will, we're late." They crossed the empty locker room and opened the door to the adjoining classroom. The meeting was already under way, but Will's thoughts were elsewhere. Seeing Myra's mother had left him feeling unsettled.

He looked for an empty seat and saw one next to Aaron Thomas, who momentarily played an air guitar, then made a passing motion, moving his hand back and forth next to his ear. It was Aaron's signature, his way of saying "Let's play ball."

Coach Boorman shot a stern glance at Will as he slid into a chair. The coach was a former lineman at the University of Colorado who, at thirty-seven, still looked and acted fit to play. He was an authority figure that no one on the team dared to challenge. He called all the plays, on the field and off. You did what he said or you didn't play, no matter how big, how fast, or how capable you were.

His talk began with his usual salvos about team spirit, pride, and honor. But this time he also said that individual goals must not interfere with the team effort. He looked right at Will when he said it. Chairs scraped against the floor as players moved in their seats. A few coughs filled the uneasy silence. Sure, Will would give up the record for the team effort, but he didn't see how not making the yards he needed would help the team.

"That said, I want the entire offense to do everything necessary for Will to get the school rushing record as quickly as possible," Boorman said. A cheer went up, breaking the tension, and players pounded their hands against their desks. "Then all we have to worry about is winning the game and the conference title. I know we can do it."

Just then, the phone in the room rang and Boorman answered it. He listened a few moments. Will was close enough to the front of the room to hear his reply. "Is it anything serious? . . . I see. I'll tell him."

He hung up. "Lansa, you're to report to the office immediately. Then get right back here when you're done with your business. You've got a game to play."

TWO

William pushed away from the desk, walked across the empty locker room, then took the stairs two at a time. He guessed it was his father calling from the reservation to say he wouldn't be able to make it to the game. Will knew that between his job and his ceremonial duties in the Bear Clan and Two Horned Society there was little time left over for travel.

But when he arrived at the office, there was no call awaiting him. The secretary at the front desk gave Will an appraising look, then pointed to the conference room. The only time students were taken to that room was when serious disciplinary actions were meted out, and usually the student's parents were on hand to witness the event. But Will hadn't done anything and the coach had told him to come right back, so it couldn't be anything like that.

He knocked on the door, and it was opened by Mrs. Tarpin, the principal. She was a stout woman with short, straight hair streaked with gray and round glasses with black frames. "Please, come in, Will."

Myra's mother and Taylor Wong, Myra's best friend, were seated on opposite sides of the table. Neither of them smiled as he entered the room. Sheriff Bower Kirkpatrick stood behind them, his arms crossed. His six-foot-three-inch frame seemed to fill the office, making it feel more crowded than it was.

"Hello, Will," Kirkpatrick said in a professional voice that was neither friendly nor accusatory. "Take a seat."

"Sure. What's going on?"

Will sat opposite Taylor, who looked as if she'd been crying. She had long ebony hair and expressive features with dark, almond eyes and full lips that made her look like she was always pouting. "Hi, Will," she muttered.

"Will, do you know where Myra is?" Laura Hodges asked. She ran a hand through her auburn hair, hooking strands behind her ear.

"No. I haven't seen her all day."

"What about last night?" Mrs. Tarpin asked, sitting down to his left. "Taylor thought you might have been with her."

"I was, for a while. We met at Ashcroft."

"Ashcroft?" Laura Hodges leaned forward. "Myra didn't say anything about going to Ashcroft. She was supposed to go to Taylor's house for the night. Now I get a call an hour ago and find out she didn't show up at school and Taylor never saw her last night."

Will recalled Myra's mentioning that she was going

to stay at Taylor's. They were going to study together for an art history test. "Didn't you call her house to see what happened to her?" Will asked Taylor.

Taylor frowned. "Myra told me she was going to see you. When she didn't show up, I just thought"— she shrugged—"that it got too late and she decided to go home."

Kirkpatrick moved around the table toward Will. "Why did you go to Ashcroft?"

"It was Myra's idea. She wanted to meet me there, so I drove over as soon as football practice ended."

Kirkpatrick stopped in front of him. "What time was that?"

He looked up at the sheriff. "About six-thirty."

It felt odd to be questioned by Kirkpatrick. Will thought of him not so much as the sheriff but as his friend's father. He had known the Kirkpatricks since middle school when he and Claude first played together. Kirkpatrick was a stern but dedicated father, who had mapped out his son's future. He wanted Claude to become an all-American tackle in college and play in the NFL by the time he was twenty-two.

"How long were you there?" Kirkpatrick asked.

"Maybe an hour. We walked around the ghost town for a while, then went back to the parking lot."

The sheriff placed a hand on the table and leaned forward. "How long did you stay in the parking lot?"

"Not long. I walked her over to the minivan. We talked awhile, then we both left." He waited for the sheriff to ask what they talked about, but he didn't.

"Did you see Myra drive away from the parking lot?"

He thought a moment. "No, I think I left first."

"You think?"

"I did leave first."

He leaned closer to Will. "Is there anything you're not telling me, Will?"

He shook his head. "No, sir."

Kirkpatrick straightened up and looked over at Myra's mother. "I'll have one of my deputies head over to Ashcroft and take a look around. Hopefully, she just went to someone else's house for the night, since you knew she was staying out, then skipped school this morning."

"I'll check the list of absentees and we'll call every one of them," Mrs. Tarpin said.

"What else can you do, Sheriff?" Laura Hodges asked. "I'm really worried about her. She's never run away."

Kirkpatrick considered her question. "With someone over sixteen, we usually wait until the person's missing for twenty-four hours, but in this case I'm going to go ahead and issue an all-points bulletin."

Myra's mother was well known in local politics. The fact that the sheriff, not a deputy, had shown up at the school to meet her testified to her influence. So did the action he was taking. But Will was glad he was doing it.

"You can go, Will. Good luck in the game." Kirkpatrick patted him on the back.

"Thanks."

As Will left the office and headed back to the locker room, he knew he should have said something about his decision to break up with Myra. After all, it might be the reason she'd skipped school. If he'd been talking alone to the sheriff or to any one of them—even Mrs. Tarpin—he probably would have mentioned it. But at the time, with everyone in the room, it had seemed a personal matter.

But where had she gone last night? That question left Will with an uneasy feeling.

THREE

Corey stepped cautiously out of the elevator and into a wide corridor. She looked to her right, her left. Along the center of the corridor were a row of computer workstations. The screens were illuminated, but no one was at the stations. She decided to go to the right and moved quickly along the wall past panels of blinking lights. She reached a green door and tried to open it. A sign flashed a message: GREEN ACCESS REQUIRED.

She moved on, then stopped by a blank screen on the wall. She tapped the access bar, hoping to gain clearance for the green door. But the screen flashed a message in red: INTRUDER ALERT.

Corey quickly moved on. She came to a corner, paused, then edged forward. She peered down the passageway on her right and saw something rushing toward her, darting right, then left. She calmly aimed her megablaster and fired at a hulking creature garbed in a bright purple and yellow uniform. The alien crumpled to the floor in a heap.

She turned to her left, but this time she was too

late. Another alien, even larger and more garishly costumed than the one she'd just eliminated, towered over her and fired its weapon. The computer screen turned into a maze of dots and through the dots a death mask appeared and the words YOU'RE DEAD.

Corey Ridder sighed, then hit the escape button. Beaten at her own game, she thought and smiled. She pushed away from the monitor and looked up at the clock. There was no one in the computer lab this afternoon. Everyone had left for the football game. She checked to make sure all the computers were turned off, then locked the door and strolled down the empty hallway. Once she was outside, she crossed the parking lot and headed for the stadium.

Even though she'd been to all the home games this year, she wasn't really a football fan. She liked playing games, not watching them. But, then, her games tended to be mental ones and mostly played on computers. After all, she was one of the tech-nerds. A female tech-nerd at that.

She went to the games for one reason: to see Will Lansa, number 42. She had a crush on Will, a bad one. It had started during the first week of school this year when she saw him walk into the computer lab while she was on duty as sysop—one of the systems operators. Every time she saw him, her feelings toward him deepened.

The teams were on the field and the game was about to begin as Corey arrived at the stadium and handed her ticket to the man at the gate. She heard the thunder of pounding feet in the stands and then the cheers as the ball was kicked off.

The other team had the ball, so she didn't care what was going on. She climbed into the stands, glad that no one paid any attention to her. Not that she ever attracted much attention. It was just embarrassing, coming to the games by herself.

She kept climbing until she reached the top row, which was empty except for a few middle school kids. Once she was seated, she felt better. Everyone was in front of her now. The crowd looked like a blur of orange and brown, the team colors. A six-foot feathery hawk, the mascot, cavorted on the sidelines near the cheerleaders.

She reached into her purse and took out a butterscotch candy and looked down at the field. The Leadville team still had the ball.

She slipped her hand into her purse again and took out her binoculars. She scanned the sidelines until she found number 42. He was standing next to number 8, the quarterback who she knew was Aaron Thomas. He was in her history class and was a real jerk, but she knew Will had to put up with him.

So did she. Aaron sat behind her and tried to copy her answers on tests, ever since he found out she was getting A's. Otherwise, he ignored her, except for the time he'd snapped her bra. She'd turned around and told him to stop it or she'd file a sexual harassment complaint. He'd muttered that there'd been nothing sexual intended, but he'd never touched her again.

Leadville was kicking the ball. Good, now she'd see Will in action. She peered through the binoculars as he trotted onto the field and into the huddle.

He looked like just one of the players now, but she knew that he was different, just as she was. They were both from families of mixed racial heritage, but it went beyond that. They were outsiders looking in, and neither of them cared much for what they saw. In her case, it wasn't just because she was black. That was part of it, but it was more complicated than that. Her interests and expertise set her apart.

Of course, if she told Charlie Baines, the other afternoon sysop, what she thought of Will, Charlie would laugh and tell her that Will was a football hero. He was popular and accepted by everyone. He'd lived here most of his life and his family was rich.

Yet, she knew Will's secret. She knew that in his heart, he was not what he seemed. Like her, he was here in this place—this school, this town—but he was not of it.

Her parents were computer consultants who had moved here a year ago from Chicago. They worked at home when they weren't traveling. They enjoyed the lifestyle of Aspen and were concerned that Corey didn't like it much and didn't have any friends. Sure, it was pretty here in the mountains, but pretty views only went so far. She couldn't wait to graduate and go away to college at the University of Chicago where she would live in a real city again. Meanwhile, there was Will Lansa.

Number 42 got the ball on the first play. He zigzagged through the players, broke free of a tackle, and raced toward the sidelines, where he was pushed out of bounds. A roar went up from the stands, and she heard the announcer say that Lansa had gained twenty-three yards.

She quickly calculated that he needed thirty-nine more yards to make the record. The fact that Will was an exceptional player hadn't even occurred to her until a couple of weeks ago when she'd heard about the record he was going to break. She figured Will ran because he had to run or he'd go crazy. It was the same way with her. If she couldn't lose herself in cyberspace, where she created worlds for players to explore, she would suffocate in this charming yet utterly pretentious place, Aspen.

She watched how Will leaned forward in the huddle, how he lined up for the play. He took the ball again, and she grimaced in agony when he was tackled after picking up three yards.

He was looking up into the stands as he walked back to the huddle. She was too far away for him to see her and even if he could, he wouldn't recognize her. The truth was, he didn't know she existed. Whenever Will needed any help in the lab, Charlie assisted him. She couldn't allow herself to get that close to him. Not yet. And there was no way she could talk to him as if he were just one of the other students in the lab.

Two plays later, Will broke free for sixteen yards,

and in the following play he gained five. He was getting close now. Fifteen yards to go. With any luck, he could break the record in a couple more plays. Then maybe they would give him a rest.

The huddle broke, and Will lined up a couple of yards behind Aaron Thomas. Will must be exhausted, Corey thought. He was carrying the ball almost every play. From somewhere below her in the stands, she heard several people call out in unison. "Do it, Lansa!"

The ball was snapped, and Aaron jammed it into Will's midsection. He lowered his head and charged through the line. But this time one of the Leadville players dove at him headfirst. Their helmets collided with a crack that even Corey could clearly hear. Will dropped to the ground.

He didn't get up. He didn't move.

She leaped to her feet and watched in a daze, her eyes fixed on the motionless figure on the field. She heard someone say it was a safety blitz. She didn't know what that meant, but she didn't see anything safe in what had happened. People rushed from the sidelines onto the field, surrounding Will, and he disappeared into the vortex.

Corey started walking. She kept walking until she was at the bottom of the stands. She saw two men with towels over their shoulders run onto the field with a stretcher. That was enough. She headed for the gate. She didn't want to see Will carried away. If he was paralyzed . . . she pushed away the thought and walked faster.

FOUR

Firelight flickered off the faces of a dozen young men and boys seated along a curving ledge, and Will realized he was among them. They were in a kiva, a circular subterranean chamber where Hopi rituals were held. Near the fire pit in the center, an old man wearing a robe was talking to them and pointing at the stars through the ladder hole above them. He was saying something about other worlds that people had lived in before entering this world. He was speaking in Hopi, a language Will did not know, but now he understood every word perfectly.

The old priest finished his talk and covered part of the fire pit with a flat rock so that there was only a faint glow in the kiva. Suddenly, a stream of men descended the ladder. They wore robes, and on their foreheads were large four-pointed white stars. One of the men was bald and his head was painted gray.

Masau, Will thought, *god of the underworld and guardian of the earth.* Masau stood off to one side of the other men who were facing the boys. The initiates.

That was it. The boys were initiates and Will was one of them.

The men with the stars were making a low humming sound and a peculiar hissing like a cosmic wind. They were spirits of the past and other worlds. For a moment, a white-robed figure emerged and said: "I am the beginning; I am the end."

The spirit sounds grew in volume and power, and the chaotic movements of the star-faced figures swallowed the one in white. The flat rock was pushed over the entire fire pit, and the kiva was plunged into darkness. Shouts erupted, the star spirits, priests, and initiates pulled off their robes and scrambled for the ladder to escape the kiva and the darkness that had enveloped the world.

In the midst of the confusion, Masau appeared in front of Will and motioned him to stand up. When he did, Masau stepped back and Will saw Myra in the center of the chamber. She was stumbling away from someone or something, a stricken look on her face, then a hand reached for her throat and a knife flashed.

Will reached out to Myra. But she was gone and he was lying on his back. Several faces, including the coach's and the trainer's, were looking down at him. He felt shaken up, groggy, and confused by what he'd just experienced.

Coach Boorman dropped onto one knee in front of him. "Can you hear me, Will?"

"Yeah."

He held up a hand in front of Will's face. "How many fingers do you see?"

Will focused his eyes. "Two."

"Where are you?"

"Where am I? On the ground. At the game."

"What day is it?"

He felt a dull ache near the crown of his head, but his thoughts were clearing. "Friday. We're playing Leadville."

The trainer asked Will to wiggle his fingers and move his feet. He did so without any problem. He sat up and saw the stretcher. "I'm okay. You don't have to carry me. I can walk."

A couple of players accompanied Will to the sidelines as the crowd cheered. He sat down on the bench and took off his helmet.

"How do you feel?" the coach asked after sending in the next play with the second-string halfback.

"Just a little dazed. Give me a couple of minutes. I'll be ready to go back in."

"No. You're out for the game. I'm not taking any chances. You might have a concussion."

"But, coach . . ."

Boorman walked away and turned his attention back to the field. Will knew that Boorman was always cautious about allowing injured players into the game and especially wary about head injuries. Will felt better already, but he knew his chances of getting back into the game were slim.

After a few moments, he turned toward the stands and gave a thumbs-up sign to his mother and grandfather, who were seated behind the bench several rows up. He searched for his father but didn't see him. Then he saw a man sitting alone with no one on either side of him. His head was bald and painted gray.

Masau.

He was smiling, but then his features shifted, his lips turned down, and his face dripped blood.

"Will!"

He turned around and saw the trainer standing over him. He felt Will's head as he asked more questions, testing his memory. Will tried to concentrate on what the trainer was saying, but now bits and pieces of what had happened in the kiva came back to him. Some kind of ceremony . . . ending in darkness and chaos . . . Masau in front of him . . . Myra killed.

"How would you describe the pain?" the trainer was saying.

"It's like a little headache. That's all."

"Take these aspirins. We'll see if that does any good. Don't jump up or even walk around. Just stay right here."

Will nodded, and when the trainer walked away, he turned back toward the stands and searched for Masau. Three girls were sitting in the space where he'd seen the mysterious being from his dream. But now he wasn't so sure what he'd seen.

The game continued on without Will, and in spite of his repeated comments to the coach and trainer that he felt fine, he remained on the bench. Without Will on the field, the team struggled, then faltered. With less than two minutes left in the fourth quarter, Leadville had the ball on the Hawks' twenty-eight-yard line and the score was tied at 14-14.

Then the ball popped free on a running play, and a half dozen players scrambled to recover it. Several Hawks leaped up in the air and pointed in the direction of the Leadville goal line. The Hawks had recovered the ball on their own twenty-five-yard line.

"Lansa, come here," Boorman shouted. Will grabbed his helmet in the hopes he'd have another chance. "Are you ready to go out there?"

"I've been ready since the first quarter," he said, his heart suddenly pounding.

"Okay, you're going in after this play. But before you get too excited, listen closely. I'm going to use you as a decoy for two plays. The defense will be focusing on you, but Thomas is going to pass."

Will's spirits sank. But he told himself he'd already conceded he wasn't going to get another chance at the record, that he'd have to wait until his senior year. He watched Aaron Thomas complete a screen pass for eight yards as the coach gave him the two plays.

"Now go out there and do your part. We're going to win this one," Boorman said.

Will raced onto the field. In spite of what he knew, it felt great just to be in the game. It was as if he'd been out of action for weeks. Then a cheer went up as his number was spotted by the crowd.

"I don't like it," Aaron said as Will told him the plays. "You should run at least one of them."

"There's not enough time for running plays," Will said. "Coach is right. Call the play."

Aaron faked a handoff to Will and faded for a pass as Will raced around the right end. He looked up to see four or five defenders just as they realized their mistake. They all pulled up short, except for a linebacker who hit him across the thighs. Will dropped to the ground, then rose up just in time to see the left end catch a fifteen-yard pass and break away for twenty more yards. Now they were on the Leadville thirty-two-yard line, but the clock was ticking.

With less than a minute left, the players raced into the huddle. Aaron called the play, but it was the wrong one. Instead of a fake handoff and a rollout pass, Aaron was going to give the ball to Will on a slant play off the right tackle. It was Will's favorite play, but it wasn't what the coach had called.

There was no time to argue. Will quickly lined up; Aaron took the snap, turned, and pressed the ball into Will's midsection.

He darted toward the line, certain the play was a big mistake. He bounced off one tackler, spun around, and then he heard a crack inside his head and everything shifted. He moved with a fluid motion and a lightness that made him feel as if he could fly. Everyone else seemed stuck in slow motion. He could see the gaping holes opening in front of him as he glided ahead. A wind whispered in his ears and seemed to propel him forward.

Tacklers and blockers fell away, and he was alone on the fifteen-yard line, the ten, the five, and then a hawk swept down in front of him, and soared away just as he crossed into the end zone. The roar of the crowd filled his ears. He held the ball up and was mobbed by his teammates.

"Did you see that hawk?" he gasped as Claude Kirkpatrick pulled him to his feet. "It almost hit me in the head."

"You're the only hawk I saw," he shouted back. "And you were flying. You flew away from everyone."

On the sidelines, Will saw Aaron run up to Boorman and shout, "Hey, coach. Great call. I thought a running play was suicide, but it worked."

Boorman didn't answer.

So Aaron had helped him get the record, but then he'd placed the blame for changing the call on Will. That was just like Aaron. He'd take chances, but if he could put the blame on someone else, he'd do it.

The players were all congratulating Will as the remaining seconds ticked off the clock. Leadville desperately tried for a comeback, but after two futile plays it was over. As his team headed to the locker room, the victory and Will's personal triumph were overshadowed by an urgent thought. He had to find out what had happened to Myra. He couldn't enjoy the victory until he knew she was okay.

FIVE

Sheriff Kirkpatrick was talking to Coach Boorman outside his office as Will walked out of the shower. He stopped a few feet away, his towel wrapped around his waist.

"Will, come over here." Kirkpatrick motioned him over and slapped Will on the shoulder. "Nice run there at the end. I guess you recovered from that knock on the head."

"I guess so."

Coach Boorman walked away. He hadn't said a word to Will since the game had ended.

"Is Myra back home yet?" Will asked.

"As a matter of fact, she's not. We've got an APB out on the minivan, so hopefully something will turn up soon."

"Is there anything I can do?"

"Not unless there's something more you can tell me about last night. Did she give you any hint that she might be going somewhere other than Taylor Wong's house?"

"No. Not a word."

Kirkpatrick shook his head. "It's a puzzler. She's not the type to run off."

Will was about to tell the sheriff that he and Myra had decided to break up, when Kirkpatrick excused himself and walked over to Claude, who'd just come out of the shower.

It didn't matter what had happened between him and Myra, Will decided. Their relationship had been faltering for several weeks and he doubted that his decision was a big surprise to Myra. Certainly it wouldn't cause her to drive off in her mother's minivan and abandon her life. It didn't make sense.

After Will dressed, he saw Tom Burke, his mother's boyfriend, waiting for him near the door of the locker room. Burke was a tall blond ski instructor and actor who possessed the good looks of a leading man. He'd had a few minor roles, mostly in skiing movies, but he was still waiting for his big break.

Burke smiled, clasped a hand on Will's neck. "Hey, great run. I got there about the middle of the fourth quarter, so I saw the best part of the game."

"Thanks."

Burke was always friendly toward Will, but he suspected it was a performance for his mother more than a genuine interest in Will. Showing up for the game at the last minute was just the sort of thing Burke would do. He could say he was there, but he didn't have to waste his entire afternoon. But Will didn't blame him. After all, Burke wasn't his father or even his stepfather.

"Your mother nearly had a heart attack when you went back in the game. She thought you should've been taken to the emergency room in the first quarter."

"That's Mom. Where is she?"

"Right outside the door, waiting for you. She wants to take you to Dr. Franks."

"That figures." Will groaned.

"I told her you'd probably want to party tonight with your friends," Burke said with a laugh.

"Yeah. I'll be right with you." Will walked over to his locker to get his equipment bag.

The burly center looked at Will, grinned, and shook his head. "I couldn't believe the coach called a running play with forty seconds left. No way, I said."

"I was lucky." Will responded, but he was watching Aaron Thomas, who had just closed his locker door a few feet away. Aaron walked away without commenting. *I'll talk to him later,* Will thought as he left.

Marion Connors beamed when she saw him. She wore jeans and a Hawks' sweatshirt, and her light brown hair was tied back in a ponytail, making her look younger than thirty-eight.

She gave him a hug and a quick kiss on the cheek. Her green eyes sparkled. "Oh, Will, I'm so proud of you. You were great. Just great. And you got your record, too." Then she frowned and lightly ran her fingers through his short hair. "Does that hurt? How does it feel?"

"It's okay, Mom. Really, I'm all right."

"I've already called Dr. Franks. He said to come right over to his office. He'll meet us there."

"I heard," Will muttered.

"C'mon. Grandpa's got the car out front."

"Do you know if Dad was here?"

"I got a call from him earlier today," she said as they climbed the stairs from the locker room. "He apologized. He got tied up and couldn't get away. He said he'd make it up to you."

She did her best to relay the information without adding her own feelings, but Will could tell his mother was disgusted with her ex-husband for not keeping his word—and she'd probably told him so.

"Mrs. Hodges also called," Marion said with a frown. "It was about Myra."

"I know. I've talked to her and Sheriff Kirkpatrick."

"And?"

"And I don't know where she is."

"You don't sound too concerned," Burke said.

"Of course, I'm concerned. As soon as we get my head examined, I want to see what I can find out."

Burke laughed. "I hope you got time for dinner. It's on me tonight. Your choice of restaurants."

"Don't worry, Will. When we get to Dr. Franks's office, I'll call Laura Hodges and see if Myra's come home," Marion said.

The visit to the doctor and dinner swallowed most of the evening. It was nearly nine o'clock when Will's grandfather finally pulled his Land Rover into the driveway of the three-story house on Ute Street. Will went immediately to his room on the lower level and picked up the phone.

Dr. Franks had said Will might have suffered a minor concussion, but as long as he didn't start throwing up there wasn't anything to worry about. The trainer had already told him as much. Will didn't tell the doctor or the trainer about the peculiar dream he'd had in the short time he was unconscious. They'd only been interested in how he felt and how clear his thinking was. If he told anyone about the dream, it would be his father. But it didn't look like Will would be seeing him for a while.

He called Taylor to see if she'd heard anything new about Myra, but her mother answered the phone and said Taylor had gone to a party at Paige Davis's house.

What party? he wondered as he hung up. Then he remembered that right after he'd told Myra his decision, she'd said something about not going to Paige's place together. She must have been talking about the party.

He didn't really feel like partying, but he wanted to talk to Taylor alone. She might know more than she was saying. Besides, maybe someone else at the party would know something.

It was quarter to ten when Will arrived at Paige's house on Red Mountain. His mother had tried to convince him to stay home and rest, as the doctor had advised, but when he'd finally promised her he'd be home by midnight and he wouldn't drink anything alcoholic, she'd reluctantly told him to go ahead.

Although it wasn't the first time Will had gone to a party at Paige's, he had trouble finding the turnoff. He passed it once before spotting the narrow drive. It wound upward for a quarter of a mile through towering aspens and pine trees and ended at a parking area next to the palatial house, which was built on four levels and had ten bedrooms and six bathrooms. The enormous picture windows on the top three levels looked out toward Aspen Mountain and the town below. Everyone was gathered in the basement, which included a game room, a swimming pool, Jacuzzi and sauna. Paige's parents were out of town, and Paige had the place to herself.

"Hey, look who's here," Claude Kirkpatrick said when he saw Will. "I didn't think you were going to make it." He threw an arm over Will's shoulder as if they hadn't seen each other for weeks.

"Neither did I," Will said, wondering why Claude hadn't mentioned the party. He saw Aaron Thomas and a couple of other football players and recognized a few other familiar faces. Then he saw Taylor and walked over to her. She moved away from the two girls she was talking to when she saw him.

"Heard anything new about Myra?"

"Just that there's nothing new," she responded. "And I'm getting really worried, Will. I don't understand it."

"I was hoping you might know something else."

To his surprise, Aaron walked up to him, a big grin on his face. He put one hand on Will's shoulder, another on Taylor's. "You know, I always thought you two would make a great couple."

"Why do you say that, Aaron?" Taylor asked. "Because we're the only ones here who aren't white? Do you think that makes us compatible?"

Aaron raised his hands. "Hey, take it easy, Taylor. I'm just complimenting you on your good looks."

. "Some compliment."

"You're just upset because you and I didn't hit it off," he said with a wide grin.

"Right." She walked off.

"Hey, chill out, Taylor." Aaron laughed, then leaned close to Will. "What did you do, send Myra to Kansas? I heard she wasn't around."

"I don't know where she is," Will said in an even voice. "You got any ideas, Aaron?"

Aaron grinned like a maniac. His eyes were glazed and hooded as if he'd been drinking, but his breath didn't give off any odor of alcohol. "I just told you mine."

"Why did you tell the coach I called that play?" Will asked.

Aaron straightened his back, tilted his head to the side. "I never told him that. I said *he* made a great call."

"You changed his play and now he thinks I'm the one who did it."

"Hey, that's the play you told me."

"No, it's not."

"What are you complaining about, Lansa? That play put you in the record books."

"That's not the point."

"Hey, you're missing out on a lot, you know." Aaron walked away.

Will wasn't sure what Aaron thought he was missing. He looked around for Taylor, but didn't see her. He moved through the crowd, exchanging greetings. He asked about Myra over and over, but no one seemed to know anything.

Most everyone, though, seemed happy—almost too happy. There was a lot of giddy laughter. Smiles seemed to stretch from one ear to the other. "We got some beer, Will," Claude said. "You want one?"

"No, thanks."

Besides the fact that he'd made a promise to his mother, he didn't really care for the taste of beer. He also knew that people of Native American heritage were susceptible to alcoholism. Whether it was genetic or not, he didn't know. But it was enough to make him wary of drinking beer or anything alcoholic.

"So what's your father think of you drinking while he's running for reelection?"

"He doesn't mind if I have a beer at home once in a while." Claude smiled. "And Paige's place is home away from home."

"Where is Paige?"

"In the Jacuzzi. I was going to join her, if I

could find where I left my swim suit."

Just then the music on the stereo stopped abruptly and was replaced by the strumming of a guitar. Aaron Thomas was seated on a stool near the fireplace. He played a couple of chords, then started singing.

Listen, Will, ol' buddy,
there's no reason to be mad.
You got your hotshot record
and you made ol' Leadville sad.

Run, run, Lansa.
Run, run, Lansa.

Listen, Will, ol' pal
about that bump on the head,
Don't take it out on me
'cause I'm the one who said:

Run, run, Lansa.
Run, run, Lansa.

Several others joined Aaron in the chorus and repeated the verse. In spite of himself, Will couldn't help smiling. Finally, he waved a hand at Aaron and walked over to the wet bar in the game room.

To his surprise, Claude Kirkpatrick was sitting by himself, his head bowed over his beer. "What's wrong, Claude?"

"You know, Aaron's the one who's playing hot-shot. Not you. You hear about the band he's going to be playing in? He's the lead singer, of course, and they're going to play some of his songs. I've heard them and I'll tell you, Will, I can write better lyrics."

"Yeah, you probably can."

Will knew Claude had a jealous streak, that he suspected Aaron was trying to steal Paige from him. Still, he was surprised by Kirkpatrick's sudden change in mood.

Claude slid off the stool and straightened his back. "Oh, forget it. Just forget it." He walked away.

Forget what? Will thought.

Just then the door to the Jacuzzi room opened. Steam filtered out and Paige Davis, wearing a bikini, stepped into the doorway. "Hey, catch! I found my dad's swim suit on the shelf in here." She threw him a pair of khaki trunks. "Oh, Will. I thought Claude was sitting there."

She started laughing, laughing too loud and too long. Then she rocked from side to side, a wide grin on her face, her wet hair plastered against her head and shoulders. "Well, don't just sit there. C'mon and join us."

"Maybe later."

"Oh, this stuff is weird. I feel like I'm melting, you know, like an ice cube." She started laughing again. "Pretty soon there won't be anything left of me." She leaned forward and smiled. Her eyes were all pupil. "I'm melting away."

She ducked back, closing the door, and Will heard

her muffled laughter. He set the trunks down on the counter and poured himself a soft drink.

"So Paige couldn't lure you into the Jacuzzi?" Taylor said as she sat on the adjacent stool.

He shrugged. "I guess not."

"I think she's on the Chill."

"What is it?"

"Some kind of new designer drug the Hollywood crowd's into. It's real expensive. Aaron was trying to get me to try it earlier."

"I never heard of it."

"It was around here last summer. There were rumors that it was coming here in a big way, then I never heard anything more about it—until tonight."

SIX

"Will, wake up, Will."

Marion Connors's voice reached him from far away and pulled him up from a deep sleep. He rubbed his face, blinked his eyes, and looked at the clock on the bed stand. It was seven-fifteen.

"Mom," he said in a gravelly voice, "it's Saturday."

"Will, there's someone here to see you. It's about Myra."

He sat up and saw his mother standing in the doorway wearing a robe. "Did she come home?"

"You better get dressed and come upstairs." The tension in her voice snapped Will wide awake.

He pulled on a pair of jeans and a sweatshirt and headed for the bathroom. A couple of minutes later, he found his mother sitting at the kitchen table with a woman about her age. She had short blond hair and wore a ski sweater that might have been purchased in the sports clothing shop Will's mother owned.

"Will, this is Stephanie Olsen. She's a detective with the sheriff's office. She wants to ask a few questions."

"What happened to Myra?"

"Sit down, Will." It was more of a command than a request. Her large green eyes searched his face as he eased into a chair.

"We found the minivan in Carbondale. It was stolen by a couple of kids who found it at Ashcroft Thursday night. They say the keys were in the ignition. No one was around, so they took it."

"What about Myra?"

"They claim they never saw her."

"Do you believe them?"

"My feeling after talking with them is that they weren't hiding anything. Neither of them has a history of violence, and they both passed lie detector tests last night."

Will thought about the implications and realized that Detective Olsen probably didn't think that Myra had run away. Something had happened to her, something bad, and Will was a suspect—maybe the only suspect.

"Do you remember Myra wearing a red scarf Thursday night?"

Will thought a moment. "Yeah, but she lost it."

"Oh, how?"

"We were inside one of the buildings. It was dark and Myra got spooked. When she ran out, her scarf came off. She didn't want to go back inside for it."

"Didn't she ask you to go get it?"

"No, she just wanted to leave. Did you find it?"

Detective Olsen considered his question a moment

before answering. "It was ripped and hanging on the edge of a protruding piece of wood."

Will's mother carried two cups of coffee to the table, one for Olsen and one for herself. She gave Will a glass of orange juice.

Olsen thanked her, then continued her questions. "What kind of mood were you in when you went back to the parking lot?"

Will felt uneasy about the questions, even though he had nothing to hide. "We just talked for a while before we left."

"Before you left. You told the sheriff you didn't see Myra leave."

"Right."

Olsen stared at him as if she were looking inside him. "Did you tell her you didn't want to see her anymore?"

A beat passed. *How could she know?* Of course: He'd mentioned it to Claude, and he'd told his father.

"Yeah, we broke up."

"Why didn't you tell that to the sheriff yesterday?"

Will shrugged. "I didn't think it was important."

"Will," his mother said, "of course that could be important. Myra was upset."

He shook his head. "Maybe. But I don't think she'd run away, especially not without the minivan."

"Unless she went with someone else," Detective Olsen said as she jotted down something in her notebook. "How'd she get along with her parents?"

"As far as I know, everything was fine at home."

Olsen never took her eyes off Will. "But things weren't so good between the two of you?"

Will stared into the glass of orange juice. "It just wasn't going anywhere. I think she knew it, too."

Will's mother came to his support. "Kids at this age usually don't have long-term, stable relationships. There's nothing unusual about—"

Olsen patted the air. "Oh, I know, Ms. Connors. I've got a daughter who's a freshman at the University of Colorado this fall and a son who's fourteen. Believe me, I know."

She pushed away from the table. "Will, I understand you drive a Jeep Wrangler. Is it the one in the driveway?"

"Yeah."

"Would you mind if I take a look inside it?"

He shrugged, glanced at his mother, then back at Olsen. "I don't mind."

They walked outside, and he unlocked the driver's door of the red Wrangler. He opened it and stepped aside for the detective. There were a couple of notebooks on the backseat, but the vehicle was otherwise empty.

The Jeep had been waiting for him when he'd returned to Aspen at the end of the summer. It was a birthday present from his mother. He appreciated it, of course, and had thanked her profusely, but after several weeks on the Hopi reservation, he couldn't help feeling guilty about the ease with which such costly gifts came to him.

He had come home with a new perspective on his life and his family's wealth. He had never thought of himself as a rich kid, especially since so many kids in town were from families with a lot more money. But after his summer's experience, he knew there was no comparing his life in Aspen with that of a Hopi kid on the reservation.

For a while, he'd actually considered living with his father. At least he'd considered what it would be like, and he knew it would mean leaving behind not only his friends and family but also his way of life. The adjustment would require a commitment that he wasn't ready to make.

Detective Olsen seemed most interested in examining the rugs on the floor of the Jeep and in the rear compartment. Will and his mother watched from a distance. "Does she really think I had something to do with Myra's disappearance? I wouldn't do anything to hurt her."

Marion put a hand on his shoulder. "Of course you wouldn't. She's just doing her job."

"Will?" Olsen called to him.

He walked over, and she asked him to open the glove compartment. "I don't think it's locked," he said. "I usually don't bother."

"I'd like you to open it, please. But you don't have to, if you don't want to, you know."

"It's okay." Will popped it open. Inside was a pack

of gum, a receipt from the hardware store, a tire pressure gauge, and an empty leather sheath.

Olsen pointed at the sheath. "What is that?"

"My grandfather gave me a knife, a Buck knife for Christmas. But—"

"Did you take it out?"

His throat constricted. "I don't think so. No, I didn't."

"When was the last time you saw it?"

"Maybe a week ago. I checked the air pressure on my tires when I filled up with gas."

He stared at the empty sheath, and his eyes glazed over as he thought about the dream he'd had while he lay unconscious on the football field. At the end of it, Myra had appeared amid the chaos in the kiva and a knife slashed at her throat.

SEVEN

Sunday morning. Flakes of snow fluttered through the gray, overcast sky making it seem even colder than it was. It was the sort of day that Corey Ridder liked to stay in bed late under a heap of blankets and quilts. But this morning she was a volunteer, one of a couple of hundred who had answered the call for assistance in the search for Myra Hodges.

They had gathered in the parking lot at the high school just after dawn, and now, an hour later, she stepped out of a van at Ashcroft on the back side of Aspen Mountain. There were four or five other vans, a dozen cars, and a couple of buses parked in the lot. Clusters of people waited to be assigned to search areas.

Corey moved through the crowd and heard one student, then another talking about Myra. How smart she was, what a good person she was, how she'd helped someone out, how no one who knew her could possibly hurt her. All this was news to Corey. She only knew that Myra was Will Lansa's girlfriend.

The truth was she was more concerned about Will. One of the reasons—maybe the main reason—that she'd volunteered was to find out if he was okay. She'd worried all day Saturday without having anyone to turn to. Sure, there were kids she could have called who would've probably known, but they'd be curious about her interest in him. They'd figure out she had a crush on Will and it might get back to him. That was the last thing she wanted.

Then she spotted Will and felt a sense of relief. He looked okay. His short-cropped dark hair was covered by a stocking cap, so she couldn't see if there was a bruise or a bandage on his head. She moved closer. His brown skin, chestnut eyes, and high cheekbones were reminders of his Hopi blood that was so out of place in Aspen.

People were coming up to him, offering their condolences, as if they already knew that Myra was dead. But when one kid congratulated him on his football accomplishments, Will just looked away as if he hadn't heard the comment. *It was the right thing to do*, Corey thought.

A man with a bullhorn began organizing groups. She wanted to be in Will's group, but she wasn't standing close enough to him and she ended up in another one. She watched him move off with his group, while hers headed in another direction, away from the ghost town.

They formed a line and moved slowly across a field,

looking not only for a body but also for scraps of clothing or anything that might be linked to Myra. A chilly wind blew across the field, and Corey stomped her feet and rubbed her hands to stay warm. She wished she'd worn gloves.

They walked for more than a mile, pausing once when someone found a discarded boot and a couple other times for scraps of cloth. The items looked as if they'd been in the field for months or maybe years, but they were collected anyhow. When a baseball cap was found, the spot was marked and the cap was placed in a separate plastic bag. The cap was in good condition and there was an emblem or a letter on it, but Corey was too far away to see what it was.

Finally, they rested and waited for another group to catch up. Then the two groups joined together and continued across the field. The search went on for the rest of the morning and was coordinated in such a way that when they returned to the parking lot they walked across another field that hadn't been searched.

Tables had been set up in the parking lot, and several women were handing out sandwiches, soft drinks, and coffee. Corey walked up to one of the tables, and a middle-aged woman told her there were ham and cheese and tuna salad sandwiches. She took one of the tuna salads and was peeling away the plastic wrapping when the woman asked where she was from.

Sometimes people asked that question because they were curious about where she had grown up. But when they didn't know anything about her at all, she suspected they were thinking that she didn't belong here.

She looked up and smiled. *I'm from God, just like everyone else.*

That was what her mother, who was black, always told her to say in such situations. But she couldn't bring herself to say it. "I live in Aspen and go to school with Myra."

"Well, that's good," the woman blurted. "Let's hope they find her alive and soon."

"I hope so, too."

Corey walked away and had just finished half the sandwich when she noticed one of the organizers conferring with two sheriff's deputies. He looked excited and was pointing toward the field behind the town. Immediately one of the men unclipped a two-way radio from his belt and spoke into it. She started to move closer in the hopes of overhearing him, but he abruptly put the radio away. Then the three of them headed for the field.

She walked over toward three girls who had been standing near the men. "Did you hear that?" one of them asked in an excited voice. "He said they found something with blood on it."

Myra was dead. Corey was sure of it. She turned away, and that was when she saw Will again. He was standing apart from everyone else and looking toward the entrance to the parking lot. She followed his gaze and saw that he was watching a man in a leather jacket who was standing next to a motorcycle and observing the activity. Corey guessed the biker was nineteen or twenty.

Will started walking toward him, then stopped about ten yards away and called out to him.

"Jerry, is that you?"

As soon as Will spoke, the man swung a leg over the seat of the motorcycle and revved it to life. Will took a couple more steps toward him before the biker sped away.

Corey gazed after him, wondering why he was in such a hurry.

EIGHT

That evening over dinner, Will told his grandfather Ed Connors about the day's events. The search teams had covered the entire area in and around Ashcroft, but the search had been called off at dusk. The big news of the day had come around lunchtime when one of the adult searchers had discovered something. The area had been quickly marked off with yellow crime scene tape, and none of the kids, as far as Will knew, had seen what it was. The rumor was that it was a blood-stained undergarment—a bra or panties—but the police weren't saying, and no one he talked to seemed to know for certain.

Will had another idea about what the searchers had discovered. "I'm kind of worried that they found my knife. You know, the one that was stolen from my Jeep." He shook his head. "I should've listened to you and kept it locked."

Ed Connors stabbed his fork into his baked potato. His hair had once been red, and while it was still thick it had faded to white. He was thin and wiry with pale blue eyes, which now looked up at Will. "Too late to think about that now. Maybe you should call the shop and tell your mother the latest."

"She probably already knows all about it by now."

Besides tending her clothing shop, Will's mother was active in civic projects and knew all the town's leaders. His grandfather liked to say that between her and Tom Burke, the two of them knew all the politicians and all the actors in town, and Connors didn't seem to like any of them. In fact, he was certain that there was a conspiracy between government officials and movie industry moguls to destroy the town—or at least what he thought the town should be like.

"Yeah, you're right about that," Connors said. "She's no doubt staying right on top of it."

As Will finished eating, his thoughts drifted back to the image of Jerry Wharton in black jeans and a leather jacket, straddling a Harley. Last year, Wharton had spent his senior year sulking on the bench after Will, a sophomore, beat him out for halfback. Jerry had once grabbed Will by the back of his neck and whispered that he just might have to shoot him in the kneecaps to get back into the starting lineup. He had said it jokingly, but Will knew it was intended as a threat. Will had ignored it, and Wharton had remained on the bench. They'd barely talked the rest of the year, but Will had always felt Jerry wanted to pay him back.

But if Jerry had something to do with Myra's death, why would he show up at the search area, allow himself to be seen, then ride off when Will called to him? It didn't make sense. But there was something about Jerry Wharton, something Will knew about him, that he was forgetting.

Just then the doorbell rang and Will answered it. Detective Olsen stood on the doorstep. "Will, I want you to come down to the station with me."

"Why?"

"What's going on here?" Connors asked, placing his hands on Will's shoulders.

"I need Will to come to the station."

"What's it about? Did they find the girl?"

"Let's just go to the station. The sheriff wants to talk to Will again. You can come along, if you like, Mr. Connors."

"You bet I will. I'll drive. We'll follow you."

En route to the station, Will wondered if they were going to show him Myra's body. Would they show it to him to see if he acted guilty or confessed?

At the station, Olsen led them into a carpeted room with a table and comfortable chairs, then she left. Ten minutes later, she and Sheriff Bower Kirkpatrick walked into the room. Olsen was dwarfed next to Kirkpatrick. Tall and rangy, he looked like an older version of his son, Claude. He shook Connors's hand, then nodded to Will.

"Thanks for coming in, Will. I appreciate it. This shouldn't take too long."

He set a paper bag on the table and reached inside. "Does this look familiar?"

It was a Los Angeles Dodgers cap. Will had one just like it, but now that he thought about it, he hadn't seen it for several days. "Can I take a look at it?"

He ran his fingers over the curved brim and noticed a slight crease in the center caused by squeezing the sides together. Tom Burke had given it to him after he'd returned from a trip to the West Coast a few weeks ago. He looked up with a glum expression. "It's mine."

"That's what I thought."

"It must have been in my Jeep. Someone took it, probably when the knife was stolen."

Kirkpatrick nodded, but didn't look very convinced.

He reached into the bag again and retrieved something wrapped in plastic. He set it in front of Will. It was a knife and the blade was caked with a reddish-brown substance.

"Is it yours?"

"Don't say anything you don't want to say," Connors said.

"It's okay, Grandpa. That looks like my knife."

Kirkpatrick waited for Will to continue, as if he expected him to confess.

"We found both of these at Ashcroft today," Olsen said.

Will looked at the knife again. "It's got blood on it, doesn't it?"

No one said anything.

Connors gestured toward the knife. "Look, Bower, if this is all you wanted to do, then you've done it.

We're leaving now unless you've got something else you want to say or show us."

"There is something else," Olsen said.

Kirkpatrick reached into his shirt pocket and took out a square of foil. He unfolded it and set it on the table. Will leaned forward and saw a small amount of a blue powder. "Do you know what that is?" the sheriff asked.

Will shook his head.

"It's a designer drug called the Chill. Traces of it were found on the handle of your knife."

"I don't know anything about that," Will said.

"You must know something about the drug. Even kids who don't do drugs know about them. Word gets around."

Will recalled that Aaron Thomas, Claude Kirkpatrick, and Paige Davis had acted as if they were high on something at the party and Taylor thought it was the Chill. "Friday night at Paige's party I heard something about it."

"Was anyone doing the drug at the party?"

Will hesitated. He didn't like being a snitch. "Maybe. I don't know. I didn't stay long."

"What about before the party? Did you know about the drug?"

Will vaguely recalled hearing something whispered in the locker room a few weeks ago. He'd thought it was about a new type of steroid. He knew that some players, including Claude Kirkpatrick, had tried them, but no one talked about it openly. A couple of years ago, two or three players had been kicked off the football team for using steroids. Will had no interest in being the biggest or strongest guy on the team. Steroids couldn't make him any faster, so he never tried to find out about their availability.

"Will doesn't take drugs," Connors said when Will didn't respond right away. "You can count on that."

"We all like to defend our children, Mr. Connors," Olsen said. "But keep in mind that we're not with them every hour of the day."

"This is ridiculous," Connors said, standing up.

"Hold on, Ed." Kirkpatrick raised a hand. "There's one way to find out if Will is telling the truth. I'd like him to give us a urine sample. If he's taken the drug within the last ten days, we'll know it."

"They can't force you to do anything, Will," Connors said, "but it might be a good idea."

"I don't mind. Like I said, I've never taken the drug."

Kirkpatrick stood up. "Good. Let's take care of that right now."

Fifteen minutes later, they left the station and headed home. "I hope we did the right thing," Connors said. "Maybe we should have had a lawyer with us."

"Why? I didn't do anything. Besides, you don't like lawyers."

"You got that right, but I don't trust Kirkpatrick, either. I don't care if he is the sheriff. He's too close to these sleazy Hollywood types and he's running for reelection, which makes it even worse."

NINE

When Will arrived at school the next morning, he felt as if he were invisible. He walked down the hall surrounded by a wall of silence. No one asked him for the latest news about Myra. No one said anything. When he reached his locker, he found a folded piece of paper sticking out. He pulled it out, opened it. The note was written in thick red ink from a felt-tip pen.

You're one for the record books all right, Lansa. They'll be talking about the killer halfback for years to come.

Your Fanz

Will frowned, crumpled up the paper, and walked to his first class. Bodies moved past him in a blur. Faces leering, then disappearing. He heard his name a couple of times, but didn't see who was talking, his mind still on the cryptic message.

As soon as he walked into chemistry class everyone looked his way, then fell silent. He tossed the wad of paper into the basket and sat down. The class began a few moments later, and he pushed away the troubling thoughts that had entered his mind.

Between classes, he noticed again that no one was talking to him. Kids he knew were turning away or acting as if they didn't see him. It was an odd switch from Friday when it seemed that everyone wanted to talk to him. Finally, he saw Paige Davis walking down the hall in his direction. She looked away and started to brush past him when he grabbed her arm. "Hey, can't you say hi?"

"Oh, hi, Will. I'm sort of in a hurry right now."

"Okay." He let go of her arm. She started to walk away, then turned back to him. "Don't you know it's all over school?" she whispered.

"What is?"

"Don't act dumb, Will. The knife. Your bloody knife. Kids are even taking bets on whether or not you'll be arrested before school's out today."

"Paige, I didn't do anything to Myra."

But she'd already turned on her heels and walked away. Suddenly, he was no longer a football hero but a murder suspect. He walked to English class in a daze and found a folded piece of paper on his desk. He opened it up and saw another note written in the same red ink.

Just another stab at fame, no doubt.
                                      Your Fanz

He slipped the piece of paper into his notebook just as Claude Kirkpatrick walked into class. He glanced at Will, nodded, but didn't say anything.

Will tried his best to concentrate, but without much luck. He spent several minutes slowly shredding the Fanz note into tiny bits of paper. Fortunately, his teachers weren't calling on him today. They probably knew about the knife, too. As he walked to the lunchroom, he felt as alone as he'd been during his first days on the reservation last summer.

Every seat was taken at the football table and that was fine with him. He found a table in the corner that was empty except for two people: Charlie Baines, the computer nerd, and a girl who was also a sysop in the computer lab. Baines glanced his way, then continued talking. As Will started eating, he overheard snatches of their conversation. They were talking about computer games—not about playing them, but programming them—and Will didn't understand a thing they said.

Baines was a short kid with messy hair and clothes that always looked slept in. He'd helped Will in the lab from time to time, and from that experience Will had decided Baines didn't bathe very often. The girl, who Baines called Ridder, wore big round glasses that kept sliding down her nose. Her curly hair fell loose around her shoulders. Every time he looked her way, she turned her head. She'd probably heard all about him, like everyone else, and was probably upset that he'd sat at their table.

But for the most part, they were lost in their own world and acted as if he weren't there. As Will was about to leave, Baines suddenly turned to him. "Lansa, don't you want Death Dream Four?" he asked amid a clatter of plates and raised voices from the next table.

For a moment, Will thought he saw the bloodied features of the haggard Masau grinning at him. He sucked in his breath and glanced away. He didn't want to believe what he'd just seen. But he had to look again. When he did, he saw Baines staring at him.

"Well, do you?"

"Is that a new game, Death Dream Four?"

Baines frowned, then pointed at Will's plate. "I said, don't you want your ice cream bar."

"Oh, no. You can have it."

Baines snatched it off his plate. "By the way, someone was screwing around on the computer system and posted E-mail addressed to you in everyone's mailbox."

He flipped through a notebook and found a computer printout. "Here it is."

Will took the paper and read:

Will Lansa raced for a record
and everyone thought he was cool.
Too bad he'll only be remembered
for killing his girl after school.

Your Fanz again

Will's fingers curled into fists and he nearly tore the piece of paper in half. "Who wrote that?"

"That's the funny thing. It looks like you wrote it yourself."

"What do you mean?"

"It was your handle."

"I didn't write this."

"Then someone must know your access code. Stop by the lab this afternoon and we'll change your code."

Will nodded and walked away.

He was never so happy for a school day to end. At the bell, he hurried out to the parking lot. He just wanted to get away from all the stares and whispers. But then he saw Claude Kirkpatrick walking toward his truck. Will had been waiting for a chance to talk to him alone. Claude was just unlocking the door when Will called out to him.

"What's going on, Will?" he asked without turning to look at him.

"You tell me. Seems like someone's spreading a lot of crap about me."

Claude turned to him, and Will saw that his fists were clenched. "What are you saying?"

"I guess you told your father that Myra and I broke up."

"So what? You weren't trying to hide it."

"I don't have anything to hide. But I'd like to know what your father told you."

"Nothing. He doesn't talk about his police business with me."

"Not even when it involves one of your friends?"

Claude rubbed his square jaw. "You know, Will, you've got a lot of nerve standing there and interrogating me when you're the one in it up to your neck."

"Hey, I thought we were friends."

"We were."

With a sudden shift of his weight, Claude slammed his fist into Will's midsection. His knees buckled, he gasped for breath. Will struggled to his feet to retaliate, but Claude was in his truck, revving his engine. He pulled away, his tires spitting bits of gravel that struck Will on his arms and cheeks.

Ten minutes later, Will drove slowly through downtown, looking for a parking space. He found a spot on Hunter Street and walked the block and a half to the Elk's Club building at Hyman and Galena where his grandfather had a corner office on the second floor. He knocked on the door, then opened it as he heard Ed Connors talking on the telephone. Connors turned in his chair, then signaled Will to come in.

Connors's desk was cluttered with books and maps that spilled onto the floor. Although he was no longer actively involved in the mining business, he still held mining rights on a couple of thousand acres in Pitkin County and owned several hundred acres.

"I'm not interested," Connors said. "I told you I

wasn't interested two years ago, last year, and I'm not interested in selling now."

Will walked over to the corner window and looked down on the crowded mall where Hyman Avenue was closed to traffic. Just across the street was the old Ute City Banque building, the one-time home of a bank and now a popular bar. He leaned closer to the window as he saw Tom Burke standing outside the bar. He was talking to two men, neither of whom Will recognized. Both looked to be in their thirties. One had a black beard and curly hair, while the other wore his hair in a ponytail. They seemed to be discussing something very intently as if they weren't just casual acquaintances. Then Burke waved a hand and walked away.

Maybe they were actors like Burke, talking about new parts. Or maybe they were a couple of special effects guys. Burke had gotten into the movie business through his father, who created special effects. Burke had learned how to blow up buildings and bridges and turn car crashes into fiery disasters. His father had wanted him to take over the business, but Burke had left pyrotechnics behind. He said it was too dangerous, but Will figured it was because Burke wanted to be a star.

Will raised his gaze and looked beyond the town toward the mountain. The snow line had crept down several hundred feet from the peak. It had snowed in town a couple of times already, but it hadn't stayed long. He'd heard that the weather phenomenon known as El Niño had been bringing unusually mild weather to the Rockies this fall, but that could change any day. Winter was just around the corner.

"These lawyers, I'll tell you, Will," Connors said after hanging up the phone. "They're so damned pushy. They want me to sell out to the Hollywood slimeballs, but I won't do it."

Will nodded. He'd heard his grandfather's anti-Hollywood spiel for years and knew he was in for another dose.

"I wish you could've been here back in the forties and fifties when this was a nice quiet town with no chichi West Coast types. They've corrupted the spirit of this town, and, you know, I wouldn't be surprised if Myra's disappearance is somehow related."

He paused and frowned at Will. "Something's troubling you. What happened at school today?"

Will shrugged. "Everyone knows about the knife, and they think I killed Myra. They're even making jokes about it and betting on when I'm going to be arrested."

Connors leaped up from his chair, paced over to the window, and stared out. "You see, that's what I mean. You're going to school with the Hollywood kids, and they're just like their parents. Here a nice young girl is missing and they're trying to make a buck on it. Just like what their parents would do, except they'd make a movie about it."

"Grandpa, some of those kids are okay."

"Sure, there may be a few decent ones, but they're outnumbered. I'm telling you, Will, money and power are everything to their parents. They're not accountable like the rest of us, and it rubs right off on their kids."

Maybe it was a mistake coming up here, Will thought. Once his grandfather started talking about Aspen and Hollywood, he just got angrier and angrier. "Grandpa, I was wondering, do you think I should get a lawyer? I mean, just in case . . ."

Connors folded his arms across his chest. "I was thinking about that today. I even made a couple of calls. "The best thing right now is to lie low and see what happens. Nobody's accused you of anything yet."

That was true, but Will had a bad feeling that that was about to change.

TEN

Will came awake with a start. He sat up, blinked his eyes, and stared out into the darkness. Something had woken him up.

He heard a thump and looked over in the corner. At first, all he saw was a blur of movement. Then his eyes adjusted to the dark. The image assumed form, shape, color, and seemed to emanate a light of its own. He glimpsed a being with a cylindrical head that was red, blue, and yellow with red buttonlike eyes and mouth. Several feathers protruded from the top. A multicolored shawl was draped over the being's shoulders, and it wore a brown kilt.

Will recognized it as a life-sized version of a kachina doll that he'd bought on the reservation, a Masau kachina carved by one of the best carvers on Third Mesa. The kachinas represented the forces of nature, and among them Masau was one of the most mysterious. He recalled his father saying that Masau was many things and one of them was a symbol of death.

Will held his breath, and his heart began to pound as the kachina moved toward him. It stopped at the foot of the bed; Will could smell a musky scent of earth. The figure raised an arm and pointed at the wall behind the bed. Will didn't want to turn and look at what Masau was pointing at, but then he felt his head shifting against his will.

The wall was gone. In its place was the dark opening of a cave. It didn't seem to matter that what he was looking at was impossible. There was no cave in his room. *I'm dreaming. Dreaming, but somehow awake.* He heard a grunt from Masau, as if he'd read Will's thoughts and approved of them.

Will slipped over the side of the bed and took a couple of steps toward the cave. The cave reminded him of the one he and his father had visited during a pilgrimage this past summer. But then he saw something a few feet inside the entrance. It was a body lying facedown. It was Myra. He took a step back, but was unable to take his eyes from the body until Masau moved into the entrance of the cave and blocked his view.

To Will's astonishment, he no longer saw a kachina, but a man wearing a cowboy hat and bandana around his neck. Not just any man. It was John Wayne. Will was so startled that it took several seconds before he realized that Wayne was holding his upturned palms out toward him. In his hands was a pile of blue, snowy powder.

Will's body jerked awake.

He was lying in bed, but he couldn't move. He wanted to get up to go to the bathroom, but he was paralyzed with a dread of the unknown, of something watching him from a dark corner. Finally, he forced himself to get up and he darted for the bathroom. He turned on the light and looked into the mirror, chastising himself. He was acting like a little kid afraid of the dark. When he returned to bed, he was wide awake. He looked at the spot where the cave had been, but only saw the wall of his bedroom.

John Wayne. John Wayne. Dream images were supposed to be symbolic, but he couldn't think of how John Wayne could be symbolic of anything related to that blue powder—the Chill—that he'd held in his hands. Will was sure that's what it was.

John Wayne. J. W. What if it was just his initials? J. W. as in Jerry Wharton.

With all that had happened in the last couple of days, he'd almost forgotten that he'd seen Wharton at Ashcroft right around the time that the bloody knife had been found. Maybe he'd have a talk with Jerry.

ELEVEN

"**W**ill, hurry. Come up here. Quick!" Marion Connors called in an excited voice from the top of the stairs.

"Okay. Okay." Will pulled on his jeans, then bounded up the stairs. It wasn't like his mother to sound excited about anything at this hour. "What is it?"

The TV was on, and she was watching a morning news show from Denver. "Sheriff Kirkpatrick is going to be on. It's live."

"Did they find Myra?"

She shook her head. "I don't know. Let's watch. Here it comes."

The familiar face of the newscaster, Amelia Fields, appeared and she briefly told the story of Myra's disappearance and hinted that there might be a break in the case. Then a line of searchers appeared on the screen with Ashcroft in the background as Fields continued talking. "Myra Hodges was an honor student who was known among her friends as someone who was always willing to listen and to help out others. But it might have been these traits that led to her abduction."

Then Fields introduced Kirkpatrick, who was being interviewed from his office. "Sheriff, can you tell us the latest developments in the search for Myra Hodges?"

Kirkpatrick was sitting behind a desk clear of all clutter except for a telephone. A computer rested on a smaller desk to one side. "Unfortunately, we haven't found her yet, and we have reason now to believe that she will not be found alive."

"I understand, Sheriff, that you did find a knife with dried blood on it that matched Miss Hodges's blood type. Do you have any suspects?"

Kirkpatrick nodded solemnly and stared at the camera as if collecting his thoughts. "Ms. Fields, I'd rather not comment on that part of the investigation, except to say that we believe we are moving closer to a resolution."

"Thank you, Sheriff Kirkpatrick, for your time this morning."

Marion aimed the remote control at the television and turned it off. "Oh, he annoys me no end. Such a showoff. He's just taking advantage of this whole thing to promote his reelection campaign."

"Mom, do I have to go to school today?"

"Yes, you do. Just don't react to any taunts and don't get into any fights. You know who you are, and you're certainly not a murderer." She put a hand on his shoulder. "Just because your knife was used in a crime isn't enough evidence to arrest you. They need a stronger link." Marion smiled. "So don't worry."

The school day wasn't much better than the one before. Will felt the stares and heard the whispers. He saw Claude Kirkpatrick in class and from across the lunchroom, but they kept their distance from each other. There was something else, too, something unexpected. Some of the kids seemed genuinely afraid of him. He could see it in their eyes.

In the afternoon, he went to the computer lab on his study hour, where he sometimes went before his regular computer class. As he sat down, Aaron Thomas stood up from one of the other cubicles and walked over to him. "I heard what happened in the parking lot. I just want you to know that I think Claude is acting like a real jerk."

Speak for yourself, Will thought. He shrugged. "It's over now."

"Listen, I'm sorry about that thing with the coach. If you want me to tell him I called the play, I'll do it."

"Forget it," Will muttered.

"Okay." Aaron slapped him on the back and walked down the aisle to his cubicle. *What was that about?* Will wondered. Aaron was tough to figure out. One moment, he could be treacherous, the next fairly decent.

He pushed away his thoughts of Aaron and logged onto the system. Three letters awaited him in E-mail. A message said: DO YOU WANT TO READ YOUR MAIL

NOW? He hesitated, then hit the letter Υ for yes.

The first message was brief and unsigned.

WILL, WILL. YOU'RE SO BAD, BAD. WE'RE SO MAD, MAD.

The second one was followed by initials.

I DON'T BELIEVE WHAT THEY'RE SAYING ABOUT YOU, WILL. I'M SURE YOU'D NEVER HURT ANYONE.
C. R.

He puzzled over the initials for a minute, but couldn't place them with anyone he knew. At the top of both notes was the word USER, but no name.

LANSA (RUNNER), his handle, was at the top of the next letter. It appeared that he'd written it to himself, but he hadn't written it at all.

I KNOW WHY, WILL,
WITHOUT A DOUBT.
SHE WASN'T TRUE
AND YOU FOUND OUT.

$\qquad\qquad\qquad$ **YOUR FANZ**

He rolled his chair back from the cubicle and waved to Charlie Baines.

"Take a look at this, Charlie."

Baines, who was wearing the same rumpled clothes he'd worn yesterday, bent over Will's computer and read the message. Then, wrinkling his nose, he studied the series of numbers, letters, and symbols above the rhyme. "Someone's got your new entry code already. That's very interesting."

"Let me show you something else." Will brought up the other two letters to his screen again. "These have the same handle: USER. Who's that?"

"Okay, these were both written on one of the generics."

"What do you mean?"

"Anyone can use a computer in here on their study hour. You're taking a computer course, so you've got a code. But if you come here on study hour and just want to use a computer, you don't get a personal code. If you want to send something E-mail, you get the generic USER handle. You can change it, if you want, but they didn't."

"So there's no way of finding out who wrote those two letters."

"Well, everyone is supposed to sign in. I'd say we get about a couple of dozen people a day using the generics. But the thing is, they don't always sign in, especially if they're only here for a few minutes."

Aaron, Will thought, *wasn't taking a computer course.* He recalled the song about him that Aaron had made up at Paige's party. It was the same sort of doggerel that had been sent to him on E-mail.

He rolled his chair back and looked down the row of cubicles. The one where Aaron had been sitting was empty now. He must have been leaving when Will arrived.

"What's wrong?" Baines asked.

Will shook his head. "Nothing." He scrolled down to the third letter. "I wonder why Fanz here doesn't use a generic."

"Maybe he or she is afraid of getting caught. Using your code is almost foolproof."

"Almost?"

Baines stared a moment longer at the screen. "Let me work on it. I'll see what I can find out."

As soon as school was out, Will drove out to a new ski resort that had just opened a few miles from town. He'd heard that Jerry Wharton was working there for his father, who owned the resort. When Will arrived, the snowmaking machines were at work on the slopes.

It didn't take long to find Jerry. A woman in the gift shop directed Will to the docking area for the cable cars. When Will stepped up onto the concrete pad where the cars were loaded and unloaded, Jerry glanced at him, then turned his attention to the control panel.

"What do you want, Lansa?" he asked, keeping his back to him.

"Why were you at Ashcroft Sunday?"

"I was out for a ride and saw all the action so I stopped to take a look." He turned to Will. "Something wrong with me stopping?"

"Why did you take off when you saw me?"

"Because I didn't feel like talking to you. You got a problem with that?"

"Do you know why we were all there?"

"I heard about your girlfriend. Tough luck."

Will thought he saw the hint of a faint smile. He struggled to keep himself from lunging at him. Instead, he changed the subject. "What do you know about a drug called the Chill?"

"What?"

"The Chill—what do you know about it?"

Jerry laughed. "Why, do you want to Chill out, Lansa?"

"So I guess you've tried it."

Jerry started to say something, then stopped. He poked Will in the chest with his index finger. "If I were you, I'd keep looking for your girlfriend and stay out of my business."

Will grabbed him by the front of his jacket. "It is my business if you had something to do with Myra's disappearance. Where is she, Wharton? What do you know?"

Jerry shoved him away with both hands. "Get out of here before I have you thrown out. I don't know anything."

Will backed away. "I hope you're telling the truth, Jerry."

As he walked away, he wondered what he'd hoped to accomplish by confronting Wharton. Even if he'd had something to do with what happened to Myra, he certainly wouldn't confess to him.

Still, there was something about Wharton he was forgetting. Something important that related to Myra. It was starting to come to him. He almost had it.

He stopped in his tracks as he saw a woman with short blond hair in blue jeans and a ski jacket standing outside the gift shop. She blended in well with the clientele of the resort. But Detective Olsen wasn't here for pleasure. She must have followed him.

"Hello, Will," she said as he approached. "What's up?" Her tone was casual, as if there were nothing unusual about her meeting him here.

There was no use trying to hide what had happened. He told her in as few words as possible about Wharton and his suspicions about him.

She didn't look impressed by his story. "What if I find out that Jerry Wharton is involved with the Chill and maybe selling a little of it on the side?"

Will looked down at the sidewalk. "That wouldn't be very good for him, I guess."

"Or for you, Will. Or for you. If you're using it, you just may have led me to your source."

"I didn't come here to buy drugs. I told you and Sheriff Kirkpatrick that I've never touched that Chill. I don't know anything about it."

"That's what you said. But I'm finding that hard to believe right now."

"Why?"

Olsen stared at him in silence until Will looked away. "Can I ask you a question, Will? Or do you want to have a lawyer present?"

"Go ahead. Ask me anything you want."

Olsen waited while a couple carrying skis walked out of hearing range. "If I had killed Myra in that parking lot and wanted to hide her body so nobody would find it, I certainly wouldn't leave it near Ashcroft. That doesn't make any sense. Where would you hide it, if you were me?"

Will jammed his hands in his jacket pockets. "I don't like that kind of question."

"Why not?"

"Because I'd never do something like that."

"But what if you did? Where would you hide her, Will?"

"I didn't hide any body. I didn't do it. I've told you that."

"Listen. It'll go a lot easier for you if you tell me the truth. Get it off your chest. You'll feel a lot better."

"I am telling you the truth."

She handed him her card. "Anytime you want to talk, give me a call."

TWELVE

There were advantages to having parents in the computer industry. Corey could spend hours surfing the Net without anyone complaining about it. It was almost as if she were expected to be proficient in several computer languages, at data transfers, programming, and even hacking—although the last wasn't a skill her parents encouraged.

Tonight, though, she was determined to put all her talents to use to pinpoint who was using Will's code to post E-mail. She was curious, of course, to find out how the person had gotten the code, but her interest extended much further than that.

It was too early to tell, but she had a hunch that it was more than a simple case of a student's prank. Someone was trying to destroy Will's life. There was a good chance that the intruder knew what had happened to Myra Hodges. Or maybe the intruder had killed her. The thought made goosebumps rise on her arms.

She tapped at the keyboard, then leaned forward as the first of the mysterious letters to Will appeared. This was the one that everyone with an E-mail address had received. But this time she'd gone into the E-mail system itself and could see Will's private E-mail code, which was not available to regular users. Even though the code had been changed, the intruder had quickly regained access.

She looked at the time the letter was sent. Seven-ten A.M. Before the first class, before almost anyone was in the school. The time element was the first thing she and Baines had discussed when he'd asked for her help. He'd talked to the custodian, who'd claimed that the door to the computer lab had been locked Monday morning, as usual, until 7:45.

She sat back in her chair and puzzled over the time and the code, trying to make sense of what she was seeing. Her thoughts drifted to Will.

There was so much she wanted to say to him, but she still felt too uncertain of herself to say anything directly. She'd taken the first step in that direction by sending him E-mail, telling him how certain she was that he was innocent. Sure, she'd only used her initials, knowing there were nine other students with the same initials. But it was a step, a baby step, but a step nonetheless.

She would never have sent the note to him at all if Will hadn't sat at her table yesterday at lunch. They'd actually eaten together and it had been Will's choice. The thought still astonished her. Not that she thought he was interested in her. She knew that his so-called pals were giving him the cold shoulder. But that was their loss. As for her, she'd hardly been able to eat a thing or even look at him. All she'd done was babble to Charlie about programming. Will had probably thought she sounded like a machine, but she couldn't help it.

She focused again on the screen. There was something wrong with the code. It took her a moment to pinpoint what it was. Too many digits. She counted them. One extra. What did that mean?

She bit her lower lip. Of course. The E-mail had come from outside the school's computer system. That explained the time it was sent. But how could that be? You couldn't send E-mail from outside the system. The school administration had restricted E-mail usage a couple of years ago after some jerks were caught using the system to buy and sell steroids. Baines had said something about it after she'd started working as a sysop.

Only someone with her own level of expertise could get into the system from outside. Unless the administration had approved an outside user. There was one way of finding out. She'd hack into the administration's file of E-mail codes. If there was an outside user, she would pinpoint who it was. It might take a while, but she was prepared to stay up all night.

THIRTEEN

That evening Will was trying to concentrate on his chemistry homework when he heard the engine of his mother's Grand Cherokee as it eased into the driveway. He'd been dreading telling her about his encounter with Detective Olsen and especially the reason she'd confronted him.

He leaned toward the door and listened to the voices in the hallway. He heard his mother and Tom Burke, but there was another voice. A quieter voice that he couldn't place. Yet it was familiar. He pushed away from his desk, then walked out of his room and over to the bottom of the stairs. He listened for the voice again and this time when he heard it, a smile spread across his face.

He bounded up the steps to the landing and looked past his mother and Burke. "Dad!"

Pete Lansa wasn't the type of man who hugged people, so Will stuck out his hand. Lansa smiled, shook his hand, then clasped him on both shoulders.

His dark eyes stared into Will's and the look of support he saw bolstered his confidence.

Will and his father were both five-foot-eight and husky. But the elder Lansa outweighed Will by about ten pounds. His shiny ebony hair brushed his shoulders, a contrast to Will's, which was shaved off an inch above his ears. "Good to see you, Son. How are you doing?"

"Well, things haven't gone too well since the game."

"Your mother called and told me all about it this morning. I took a plane from Flagstaff as soon as I could."

"Tom and I just picked him up at the airport," Marion said.

"You didn't have to come, Dad. I didn't do anything wrong."

"I know you didn't. But you still need all the help you can get."

"There's something you don't know, Will," Marion said. She spoke calmly, in an even voice, but Will could tell she was tense and nervous.

Just then the front door opened and Will's grandfather walked into the house. Will knew he'd just come back from the Ute City Banque where he'd probably had a drink or two with his friends. When his gaze settled on Lansa, he frowned, then a smile spread across his face. "Well, look at this. Pete Lansa. Good to see you. How come nobody told me about this?"

"Well, I wasn't sure Pete could make it, Dad," Marion said, sounding somewhat uncomfortable. "Why don't we all go sit down at the dining room table."

Talking in the dining room meant that whatever needed to be said was important. After they were seated, Will's mother got right to the point. "This morning at about nine o'clock I got a call from Sheriff Kirkpatrick. He told me that your urine sample tested positive for the drug that was on the knife."

Will leaped to his feet. "But that's impossible. I've never taken it."

"Will, please, sit down," Marion said firmly.

"It could be a mistake," Lansa said. "You may not have been the only one tested. The samples could've gotten mixed up."

No one said anything for a moment.

"I want to take you to a lab where we can get a second test," Lansa said. "If it turns out negative, we'll have something to counter their evidence with."

"I don't like any of this," Will said. "I wish it would all just go away."

"If they're so damned sure it's Will, then why haven't they arrested him?" Connors asked.

"That's a good point," Lansa said. "They're being cautious. They want more evidence and a body."

"There's something that stinks about this whole thing," Connors muttered.

"What puzzles me is why they haven't taken you in for more questioning," Lansa said.

"I *was* questioned again—by Detective Olsen after school. Over at the Wharton Resort."

"What were you doing there?" Marion asked.

Will explained what had happened.

"That was a mistake, Will," Lansa said before Will's mother could say anything. "You just made Olsen more suspicious. You should have told her about Wharton and let her talk to him."

"Why didn't you tell me about it?" Connors asked. "You said you stayed late at school."

"I didn't want you worrying or getting mad, Grandpa."

"Well, I'm a little mad right now, boy. I believe that you're a good kid, that you're innocent, but you can't go around doing stuff behind our backs."

"I thought you trusted me." Will's voice sounded shrill.

"Your grandfather is right, Will," Marion said. "You're only going to get yourself in more trouble by pulling stunts like that."

Lansa raised both hands and patted the air. "Let's go over everything, starting with your last evening with Myra."

For the next half hour Will told his father all that he could recall. He even mentioned the misunderstanding he had with Coach Boorman about the last play of the game and Aaron Thomas's role in it. Lansa listened closely and asked a few questions.

After Will described the search at Ashcroft, Lansa stopped him. "It's strange that your cap and knife were found there, but no body."

"That's a large area," Tom Burke said, speaking up for the first time.

"But you'd think a body would be easier to find than a knife."

"Do you think she might still be alive, Pete?" Connors asked hopefully.

"I don't know. It just seems that if a person is concerned about hiding his involvement in a crime, he doesn't toss his knife into a field that is sure to be searched or let his hat blow away. That is, unless it was someone else's hat and knife and he intentionally left them behind to be discovered."

"But why would the body be hidden?" Marion asked.

"Fear, guilt. Or maybe the killer was concerned that the body might provide leads that would point to him."

"What kind of leads?" Marion asked.

"The killer's hair or his blood," Lansa responded.

"So where do you think it would be hidden, if not at Ashcroft?" Burke asked.

Lansa was quiet for a moment. "A place that seems safe, a place the killer knows."

Will thought about the cave in which he'd seen Myra's body. But the cave was just part of a dream with John Wayne, Myra, and Masau. Still, he wanted to talk about his dreams, about Masau. If anyone could help him understand what they meant, it was his father. He would wait until they were alone.

FOURTEEN

En route to school the next morning, Will imagined Sheriff Kirkpatrick and several deputies were preparing to arrest him in the parking lot. The entire student body would be gathered eagerly, anticipating his arrival, and then, as he was handcuffed and escorted away, they would all applaud.

But when he pulled into the parking lot, it looked just like any other morning. He walked to his locker, then to class, without incident. But everything seemed unreal. He was just going through the motions of attending classes while he waited. It would be horrible, of course, to get arrested and be charged with murder. But the waiting was almost as bad.

His father had told him he was going to stay in Aspen as long as it took to clear Will's name. Will knew it was a sacrifice for him to make such a commitment. He would have to make arrangements for someone to take over his duties on the reservation. He might even have to take a leave of absence. Besides, the world of Aspen was alien to him. He didn't like the closed-in feeling he got in the mountains and all the up-and-down driving. Not only was his own life being pushed aside, but he also had to face his past. Even though his parents seemed to be getting along, Will knew that it must be a strain for both of them.

Chemistry class began with a test about yesterday's lesson. He hadn't finished his homework, and now he was confusing the valence powers. Fortunately, his grades were good enough so it didn't matter if he did poorly today.

The rest of the morning went smoothly until he stopped at his locker between classes and saw Claude talking with Paige in front of her open locker across the hall. She was moving her hands and shaking her head, as if she didn't agree with what Claude was telling her.

"So what do you think they're talking about?" Taylor stopped at his side.

"Hi, Taylor. I don't know, but they've been avoiding me like the plague."

"They know something about Myra. I'm sure of it."

Just then Paige slammed her locker door. "What makes you think so?" Will asked, watching as Paige walked away, with Claude trailing after her.

"Because Paige is acting, like, real strange. I feel like I don't know her anymore. Oh, great. Here comes my worst nightmare."

Aaron Thomas walked up to them. "Hey, what's going on here? Is it a conspiracy or do you need more than two people for that? I forget."

"Good-bye, Aaron," Taylor said. "Talk to you

later, Will."

"I don't get it," Aaron said as Taylor hurried away. "What did I ever do to her?"

"Did you try to get her to take that drug, the Chill, at the party Friday night?"

Aaron was caught off guard, but only for a moment. "No way. I'm naturally high, man. Gotta go. And, hey, stay out of trouble, will ya?"

He used to think that Aaron's cockiness was a good trait in a quarterback, that it helped the team spirit. But now Will just figured Aaron was a jerk.

Taylor was the only one of his old friends who still accepted him. He was glad of that, but he wondered if Taylor might know something she wasn't telling him about Myra. After all, she and Myra had worked together last summer at Taylor's folks' ice cream shop, and one of the last things Myra had said to him was that she wanted to tell him something about last summer.

That afternoon, Will went to the computer room again on his study hour. He slipped into a cubicle and typed his entry code. His stomach knotted as he saw he had E-mail. He considered just ignoring the mail, but thought better of it.

He hit the enter key. There only was one letter.

YOU MUST HAVE BEEN REALLY MAD WHEN
YOU FOUND OUT YOUR MOTHER'S
BOYFRIEND WAS MESSING WITH MYRA

WHILE YOU WERE GONE LAST SUMMER. IF
YOU HAD ANY GUTS, YOU WOULD'VE KILLED
HIM, NOT HER.

YOUR FANZ

"What?" he said aloud and reread the note. Burke.
Tom Burke? No, it couldn't be.

"Hey, Will."

He jumped in his seat, spun around. Charlie Baines
was standing behind him, peering at the monitor over
his shoulder.

"Sorry, Will. I didn't mean to scare you. Did you get
another letter from your mysterious correspondent?"

Will tapped the delete button, erasing the letter
before Baines read it. The message had struck so
deeply that he wasn't ready to share it with anyone.
"Yeah. More of the same garbage."

Baines nodded. "I saw you come in and thought
you'd like to know what I found out."

"Did you figure out who got my code?" Will
asked, trying his best to sound casual.

"I narrowed it down to six people. Well, five really, because I'm one of them and I didn't do it,"
Charlie said with a grin. "You see, the sysops are the
only ones who have access to the student codes besides
the school administrators, and I don't think they'd be
writing rhymes to you."

"Who're the others?"

Baines held out a piece of paper with five names on

it. Will didn't know any of them, but noticed one of them had the initials C. R. Corey Ridder. "I've talked to every one of them. They all say they didn't do it, of course, and to tell you the truth, I believe them. None of them has anything to gain from harassing you."

Charlie pointed to the list. "These three had heard about Myra's disappearance, but didn't connect you with her." He moved his finger down the list. "This one knows who you are and actually went to one of the games this year, but he was in San Francisco at a computer convention over the weekend. He didn't get back until Monday afternoon."

"What about the other one—Ridder?"

Baines ran a hand through his mussed hair and smiled wryly. "Ridder lives in her own world. She's barely in contact with the other sysops, much less anyone else in this school. She's bright, real bright, but she's too focused, if you know what I mean."

Will shook his head. "I don't."

"What I'm saying is that I'm not even sure Ridder knows this school *has* a football team. In fact, earlier this fall I had a computer football game up on my screen and she asked me the dumbest questions about it, like what's a first down—that sort of stuff." He laughed. "So I don't think Corey is Fanz."

She probably wasn't the C. R. who had written him, either. "Thanks, Charlie."

"Sorry I can't be more helpful right now. But if I come up with anything else, I'll let you know."

FIFTEEN

Heading home from school, Will mulled over his latest E-mail from Fanz. It was probably just a sick joke, but whoever was playing it knew something about his home life. Fanz definitely knew about Burke and that Will had an uneasy relationship with him.

He pulled into the driveway of the house. His grandfather's Land Rover was gone, but his mother's Grand Cherokee was here. That didn't mean much, though, since she usually walked to her shop.

"Anyone here?" he called out as he stepped inside. "Dad?"

No answer. Even though his father had planned to stay in a motel, Will's mother had insisted he move into one of the spare bedrooms. He wondered if his father and grandfather were out together. He had a hard time imagining what they would talk about.

He went downstairs to his room and found the card that Detective Olsen had given him. He decided he would tell her about the Fanz E-mail and see if she could sort it out. Maybe it was just a bystander trying to make his life even more difficult than it already was. But then again, it could be someone intricately connected to everything that had happened during the past few days, someone who thought there was no way Will or anyone else would catch him. That's what bothered him. Fanz didn't seem the least bit concerned about being detected.

He dialed the number. The dispatcher answered, then transferred the call. Suddenly Will realized he didn't have any of the letters, and he wasn't sure he could retrieve them, either. He should have printed them out. Especially the last one. What if Fanz was telling the truth about Burke?

"Detective bureau," a man answered, then told him Olsen was out of the office. He wanted to take a message, but Will didn't know what to say. He hung up.

He walked upstairs and crossed the living room into the kitchen. He took out a can of Coke from the refrigerator, popped it open, and took a sip.

"Will!"

His throat constricted and the fizzy drink sprayed out of his nose. He coughed, wiped his mouth. "Tom, I didn't know you were here."

Burke stood near the picture window that spanned the wall of the dining area. He was staring out toward the slope on the opposite side of the valley. He turned and strolled toward Will. His hands were jammed into the pockets of his loose slacks. He wore a V-necked sweater, and as always his thick blond hair was perfectly arranged. He must have walked over from his apartment, but Will couldn't recall ever seeing him here when his mother wasn't home.

"I'm waiting for your mother. She asked me to go grocery shopping with her. Sounds like fun, huh?"

"Didn't you hear me when I came in?"

Burke mounted a stool along the counter that separated the kitchen from the dining area. "Sort of. I was snoozing on the couch. You woke me up."

"Do you know where my father is?"

"Nope. I haven't seen him or Ed."

Will always felt vaguely uneasy when he was alone with Burke, and now, after the last note from Fanz, he felt wary and suspicious. "I'm going downstairs to study for a while."

"Wait a minute, Will." Burke slid off the stool and walked over to him. "Tell me what's been going on. Is there any news about Myra?"

For a moment, he was tempted to confront Burke about the notes, but decided against it. "Nothing that I know about."

"How's it going in school?"

Will shrugged. "Everybody either ignores me or acts as if nothing ever happened."

"It must be hard to keep your thoughts on your schoolwork."

Burke was being more chatty with him than he'd been in some time. "Actually, it helps me forget about all of this stuff for a while."

Burke laughed. "Escaping into your studies rather than away from them. That's a twist."

"Yeah."

Suddenly, Will recalled looking down at Burke from his grandfather's office window while Burke was talking to a couple of men outside the Ute City Banque. He mentioned it to Burke. "Were they friends of yours?"

Burke blinked several times. His features stiffened, and it seemed as if he were having a hard time forming words. "I don't remember talking to anyone outside the bar."

"One guy had a ponytail. The other one had a dark beard."

"Oh, wait a minute. Those guys. Sure, I gave them directions to the airport."

Will thought Burke was lying. "Well, I better get started on my homework." He headed for the stairs again. Burke followed him.

"Listen, I want you to know something. I don't have any problems with your father being here. I liked talking to him last night. He's an interesting man."

Will paused at the top of the stairs. "Good. I'm glad he's here."

"Will, there's something important I need to talk to you about. Now is as good a time as any."

He waited for Burke to continue.

"We don't get a chance to talk very often. I mean, just you and me. I know you don't think of me as a father and I can understand that. A stepfather for a teenager is almost always awkward."

"But you're not my stepfather."

Burke didn't answer, and suddenly Will knew that his mother and Burke were planning on getting married. The realization triggered something in him and the words burst from his throat. "Did you ever see Myra while I was gone?"

The air around him suddenly turned cold as Burke's icy stare held his gaze. "What are you talking about, Will?" His voice was low and soft. "The only times I ever saw her was when she was with you."

"You never saw her last summer?"

Burke shook his head, looking puzzled. "Jeez, Will. Give me a break. Where did you come up with this?"

Will's throat tightened. He pushed past Burke and bolted toward the front door.

"Hey, wait!" Burke raced after him.

Will jerked open the door and nearly knocked over his mother, standing there with her keys in hand.

"What's going on?" she asked.

Will sucked in a breath of air and a familiar scent of perfume. He didn't know what to say.

"I'll tell you, Marion," Burke said. "We've got a problem here."

She looked between the two of them.

"You're not going to believe what Will just laid on me."

"Let's go inside," she said and closed the door behind her.

They walked over to the kitchen counter. Marion put her purse down on a stool and turned to Will. "Okay, I'm waiting. What is it?"

He told them about the E-mail messages he'd been getting and described what the last two had said.

"Who's writing this stuff?" Marion demanded when Will had finished.

"I don't know. I've been trying to find out."

"I can see how you might be upset, but you don't really believe Tom was seeing Myra, do you?"

Will realized he'd been letting his imagination run wild. He shrugged, feeling foolish and embarrassed. "I guess not. No."

"I'm thirty-five, Will. If I'd been messing around with a sixteen-year-old this past summer, you know I'd be the first one the cops would be questioning. Hell, they'd be on my trail day and night."

"That's right," Marion said. "I don't know who's done this to you, Will, but I'd like to take the little jerk's computer and throw it off a mountain right after him."

Will nodded, regretting that he'd said anything about it. He didn't know what to think anymore.

SIXTEEN

Little Annie's Eating House in downtown Aspen was one of the few places left that wasn't chichi. (That was Ed Connors's term for pretentious, expensive dining.) The atmosphere was relaxed and casual. The place was dimly lit and noisy at times, with the kitchen activity spilling into the dining area, but the waiters and waitresses were friendly and the food was good. In Will's opinion, it was the best restaurant in town.

Will, his father, and grandfather found a table in the corner away from the kitchen and after several people had greeted Connors, a waitress left them menus. Lansa studied it, but Will and his grandfather already knew what they were going to order.

"I'm glad you've allowed me to take you out to dinner tonight, Pete. I know that when you and Marion were married, I acted like a horse's ass sometimes. Well, maybe more than sometimes. I wasn't a very good father-in-law."

Lansa put down his menu. "It's okay, Ed. I wasn't exactly expecting a warm welcome in those days."

"Well, I've learned a lot since then. I'd take you as a son-in-law any day over these rich Hollywood snobs who've destroyed this town."

"Thanks," Lansa said in a noncommittal tone.

"Dad, can you tell me now what you've been doing today?" Will asked, hoping to steer the conversation away from his grandfather's obsession.

"I went to Ashcroft earlier this morning and had a look around," Lansa said.

"What do you think?" Connors asked.

"Well, I can understand why Will hasn't been arrested. The scenario doesn't work. It's even more implausible than I'd imagined."

"What do you mean?" Will asked, feeling encouraged.

"The sheriff's got a big problem, and I think he knows it. Not only is the body missing, but so is the blood. If Myra was stabbed at Ashcroft, there would be more blood than what was found on the knife."

"What's that mean for Will?" Connors asked.

"It's the key to his innocence. If Myra wasn't killed in Ashcroft or in the surrounding fields, then she was killed either inside a vehicle or somewhere else. Will's Jeep is clean. Same with the minivan Myra was driving. It would mean that Will took Myra somewhere else, killed her there, then drove back to Ashcroft to dispose of the knife in a field where it would most likely be found, thus incriminating himself."

"Of course," Connors crowed, then lowered his

voice. "It doesn't make any sense at all."

The waitress appeared with their drinks and they ordered their meals: steaks for Connors and Lansa, a cheeseburger and fries for Will.

Lansa sipped his soft drink and continued.

"It looks like the knife was planted. I think any decent detective would suspect the same thing."

Connors nodded. "Any ideas on where the body might be?"

"I had a dream Monday night that Myra's body was in a cave," Will said.

Both men looked at him. "What else did you see?" his father asked.

He wanted to say that the dream had begun with the sensation of waking up and finding Masau in his room. But the kachinas were sacred to his father and speaking of one of them in such an offhand way might offend him. It wasn't the right time, not here with his grandfather present. But there was something else he could say.

"I saw John Wayne standing by the entrance of the cave."

"John Wayne!" Connors chortled. "He didn't kill her."

"But his initials are J. W.—Jerry Wharton. That's why I went to see him the next day."

"I don't know why you'd dream about John Wayne, but I don't think the idea about the initials is right," Lansa said.

"Why not?" Will asked.

"This afternoon I had a talk with Detective Olsen. She talked to Wharton after you left the ski resort. He's got a sound alibi. He went to a movie Thursday evening and three people were with him."

There was still something about Wharton that Will couldn't remember, but maybe it didn't matter now. If Jerry had been at a movie, he couldn't have killed Myra.

"Did Olsen say anything else helpful?" Connors asked.

"She's trying to link Myra's apparent murder to drugs, but she's having trouble figuring out how Myra fits in, unless she knew something about someone she wasn't supposed to know." Lansa leaned over the table toward Will. "Any ideas who that might be?"

Will shook his head. "If I knew who was sending the E-mail to me, it might help." His mother had already told Lansa and Connors about the cryptic messages. Burke had done his best to dispel any doubts about his innocence.

"The problem is that she's getting pressure from above to make an arrest."

"Our mayor is probably behind it," Connors said. "He hates negative publicity."

To Will, it looked like Olsen was looking for a way to arrest him and charge him with murder.

Their dinners came, and as they ate they avoided talking about Myra's disappearance or Will's predicament. When they were about to leave, Detective Olsen stepped through the doorway, accompanied by two men. They took a table near the rear. The place was crowded now and Olsen hadn't looked their way. As they left, Will stole another glance at the men at Olsen's table. They looked familiar to Will, but at first he couldn't place them.

"Well, I'm going down to the Ute City Banque for a nightcap," Connors said as they paused outside. "I'm sure you two have plenty to talk about."

As soon as his grandfather mentioned the nightcap, Will recalled that he'd seen the two men outside the bar talking to Tom Burke. If they'd just been asking directions to the airport, as Burke claimed, they hadn't gotten around to leaving yet. And what were they doing with Olsen?

As they walked away, Will told his father about the two men and their apparent connection to Burke and Olsen. "It's a small town, Will. People bump into each other."

Will wasn't satisfied with that explanation, but he didn't say any more about it. As they continued on through downtown, Lansa occasionally peered into shops, but showed no interest in stopping at any of them. When Will pointed out his mother's clothing shop on Cooper Avenue, Lansa paused and looked at the window displays.

"Nice," he remarked as they walked on in the direction of City Market.

Half a block later, they reached a small plaza, and

Lansa asked Will if he wanted an ice cream cone.

Will hesitated a moment. The espresso and ice cream bar was where Myra had worked part-time. "Sure."

When they entered the shop, Will saw Taylor Wong working behind the counter. Her parents owned the place, and Taylor worked here a couple of nights a week.

He greeted Taylor and introduced his father. "Nice to meet you, Mr. Lansa. I hope you're enjoying Aspen." There was a slight hitch in her voice as she realized he was probably here because of his concern for Will. She quickly asked what they would like.

As she prepared an espresso and a chocolate cone, Will thought about Jerry Wharton again. *Jerry and Taylor.* That was it. Myra had told him that Jerry had been going out with Taylor this past summer. There was something else, too. He thought back to an evening earlier in the fall when he and Myra had been on their way to a movie.

She'd said that Wharton had hung around the shop a lot with Claude Kirkpatrick. He'd been about to ask her what Kirkpatrick was doing there when she'd changed the subject and he'd forgotten about it. Now he wondered what Claude had been doing there.

Taylor handed him his cone. He wanted to talk to her, but he couldn't do it now. There were too many customers and she might not be willing to say anything with his father present.

After Lansa paid Taylor, he and Will walked outside

and sat on a bench. The temperature had warmed to the low sixties during the day and it was still mild out.

"It's a nice town," Lansa said.

Will pushed away the disturbing thoughts that had entered his head. "Yeah, but you know what? I think about the reservation a lot. It's strange, but I really think I miss being there."

"We don't have all the stuff you've got here."

"I know, but I've been thinking that all the stuff doesn't matter so much to me anymore. I just miss being on the mesa and looking out over the desert. There's a certain feeling there. I don't know how to describe it, but it's something special."

"It's probably how the first Hopis felt when they arrived. They knew they'd reached their spiritual homeland and the great migration was over."

"Where were the people before the migration?" Will asked.

Lansa sipped his coffee. "I think you know that in our myths, it's said that Masau guided the people from the previous world into this one."

Will had expected him to say Siberia or Asia and was surprised to hear his father mention Masau. He took it as a cue that it was time to tell his own tale. "Dad, I've been having dreams about Masau. More than just dreams, actually."

His father's face was impossible to read. "Tell me about them."

Will began by describing the dream he'd had while

he was unconscious at the football game, and how, later in the game, an image of Masau had appeared to him in the stands. He described all the incidents and ended by saying that the John Wayne character in his dream Monday night had begun as Masau.

"Masau is a powerful being," Lansa said. "He's known to enter dreams and to change his appearance. I'm not surprised you thought you were awake during some of your dreams. That's another one of Masau's tricks."

Will frowned. "But is Masau real?" He knew it didn't come out right, but he didn't know any other way of saying it.

"Masau is real, but real in a different way from you and me. In one sense, he's a projection of something inside us, a part of us related to the primal spirit of our people, and maybe to all people. But in another sense, he's an independent being, a trickster who cavorts through our world and penetrates our lives in very strange ways."

Will wasn't sure he understood what his father was saying, except that he knew his time on the reservation had awakened something within him he wasn't sure he liked. "What do you mean?"

"As I've told you, Masau is many things, including a god of death. So I'm not surprised that he appeared to you when there was death nearby."

The ice cream, which Will normally craved, tasted like chalk in his mouth. "I feel like I'm responsible. I should've waited for Myra to leave before I drove away from the parking lot."

"You might have been able to prevent it from happening at that place and that time. But you couldn't be with her every moment of the day. Her death is not your fault."

Lansa stood up and tossed his empty paper cup in a trash can. Will did the same with the remainder of his cone. They started walking back to Will's house. "But why did I have these dreams? That's what I want to know."

"That's another matter. We'll talk about that later."

"But I want to know now."

They continued on in silence past City Market, then turned right and headed down Original Street toward Ute Street and the house. "You were selected, Will."

"Selected? What do you mean?"

Lansa looked up at a row of expensive condominiums. "Last summer when we went on the pilgrimage to Kisiwu, you attracted Masau's attention."

Will nodded. He hadn't forgotten his frightening experience inside the cave at the Spring of the Shadows or the peculiar dreams that had followed.

"You were chosen then to be initiated into the tribe. Do you understand?"

"But I came back here."

"That doesn't matter. When Masau selects you, the initiation will take place regardless of where you are or what you're doing."

"But why now?"

"Because it's Hawk Moon, or the Initiates' Moon. The first initiation ceremony is taking place right now as part of *Wuwuchim*."

When Will had arrived at the reservation, he'd known almost nothing of the Hopi ceremonies. But he'd soon learned about the annual cycle of dances and rituals, and now he recalled that *Wuwuchim* was the first of the three winter rites. It was also the time of the year when the kachinas returned to the Hopi mesas after spending the summer months in their home in the San Francisco Mountains.

The conversation and his thoughts about intimate Hopi matters seemed out of place in Aspen. Just the sight of people in expensive designer clothing passing by left Will feeling as if he were caught between two worlds, a part of each, yet alienated from both of them.

"What you saw in your dream was the third day of *Wuwuchim* when we smoke over the *pahos* that have been made on the first two days," Lansa said. "After that the *pahos* are taken to shrines and then the crier chief publicly announces the beginning of *Wuwuchim* from a rooftop."

Will remembered the *pahos,* or feathered prayer sticks, he had taken into the cave at Kisiwu and how concerned his father had been about where he had placed them.

"But in my dream, I saw Myra. What did that have to do with the ceremony?"

"Nothing and everything. Masau showed you the event that would be your challenge. In order to continue with the initiation, you must overcome the obstacles you face."

As they neared Will's house, one question lingered, and no matter how much he wanted to push it aside, he knew he must ask it. "Dad, did Masau have something to do with what happened to Myra?"

Lansa shook his head. "Masau is not God. He may see death, but he doesn't create the circumstances that lead to it."

That didn't make Will feel any better. It just meant that his vision was telling him what he and everyone else already suspected: Myra was dead.

SEVENTEEN

Taylor was peering into the mirror on the inside of her locker door when Will walked up to her, intent on getting answers. Her eyes widened, she turned around, and put a hand to her throat.

"Will, you startled me sneaking up that way."

"I wasn't sneaking. You got a minute?"

She closed her locker, and her eyes darted right, left, then back to Will. She looked annoyed. "Walk me to my class. There're too many big ears around here."

"Is something wrong?" he asked as they headed down the hall.

"It's nothing. Just that, well, word has gotten around that I'm still friendly with you. Even Mr. Boorman, my history teacher, said I shouldn't be seen with you. That it didn't look good."

"Boorman said that?" Will felt a sinking sensation in the pit of his stomach as he realized his coach had turned against him. "What else did he say?"

She hugged her books to her chest as they continued at a slower pace. "He said you played the game Friday even though you knew Myra was missing and that you changed the play at the end so you could get your record. He said it looked real bad for you, that you had drugs in your blood and that you'd lied to the sheriff. He couldn't understand why you hadn't been arrested yet."

Will's throat tightened; his voice cracked as he spoke. "When did he say that?"

"After class yesterday."

"I know it looks bad, but—"

"I believe you, Will. I don't think you'd hurt Myra."

"You may be the only one around here who still believes me. Maybe I should just call you tonight. There's something I've got to talk to you about."

She stopped and turned to him. "No. Ask me now."

It seemed everyone in the hall was staring at them. "It's about last summer when Myra was working with you at the shop. You were going out with Jerry Wharton, weren't you?"

"You don't think he had anything to do with what happened to Myra, do you?"

"Should I?"

"Jerry's really okay, Will. He's just stubborn, and he holds grudges too long."

Will nodded. "I'm not concerned about him. But I remember Myra saying something about Claude Kirkpatrick hanging out at the shop with Wharton. Did Claude go out with Myra while I was gone?"

Taylor took a deep breath, then slowly exhaled as she nodded. "She didn't want to tell you. She thought you'd take it wrong."

"So she was seeing him."

"For a while, but she just wanted to forget about it. It didn't work out."

"Was Claude doing the Chill? You told me it was around last summer."

Taylor glanced over Will's shoulder at someone passing by. "I think so," she whispered. "Claude and Jerry wanted us to try it. That was when things started to fall apart with Myra and Claude, because we didn't want anything to do with it."

Myra must have wanted to tell him about her and Claude when she'd mentioned him coming to the shop. But she'd changed her mind, maybe thinking that he would be jealous. Or maybe it was something else. "Taylor, you don't think Myra was . . ."

"Pregnant?"

The word hung in the air, twisted and turned in Will's mind. His head pounded. His face felt hot. Was that what this was all about?

"No, I'm sure that wasn't it," Taylor said. "She would've told me. Besides, I don't think things ever got that far with her and Claude. But something was on her mind, something she couldn't even tell me."

He remembered that Myra had wanted to tell him something before he'd said it was over between them. "What do you think it was?"

Taylor shook her head. "I wish I knew. I've got to go. I'm going to be late."

Will hurried to class, his thoughts on Claude Kirkpatrick. He would see him at lunch and confront him.

All morning, Will considered how he would approach Claude, what he would say. He didn't want to make any accusations, but it was going to be difficult to ask him about his relationship with Myra without doing so—especially after what happened in the parking lot after school the other day.

Finally, when it was time for lunch, Will hurried out of class at the sound of the bell. He wanted to catch Claude before he entered the lunchroom, so he waited across the hall.

It wasn't hard to spot Claude's curly head of hair towering above everyone else. He was walking with Paige Davis. Tall and graceful, her long neck was arched as she listened to Kirkpatrick. Will stepped in front of the pair. "Claude, I've got to talk to you about something."

"Hey, I'm sorry I lost my head Monday. It was all my fault."

"It's okay. That's not what I want to talk to you about."

"Let's go sit down and eat lunch. Nobody is keeping you away from our table."

Our table. As if he and his buddies owned it. "I'd rather talk to you here, alone." He looked at Paige, hoping she'd cooperate.

But she held her ground. "If it's about Myra, I was her friend too, you know."

"Suit yourself." He turned to Claude. "Why didn't you tell me you were going out with Myra last summer?"

Claude shrugged. "It wasn't any big deal. I figured she would mention it when she started seeing you again. We just went out a couple of times. Did Taylor tell you about it?"

"Yeah, and she told me you wanted Myra to take the Chill with you."

Claude's expression turned sour. "No way. I don't think I'd even heard of that stuff back then."

"But he knows about it now," Paige said and laughed.

"Have you tried it?" Will asked, even though he knew the answer.

Claude shrugged again. "A couple of times. So what?" He glanced toward the lunchroom. "Any more questions, Will? I'm getting hungry, smelling the food."

"Yeah. C'mon and join us," Paige said. "You know we're all pulling for you."

"That's right," Claude said. "No one wants to see you in trouble."

Will hesitated, not certain what to do. Then he saw Charlie Baines standing off to the side, looking intently in his direction. "You guys go ahead. I'm not very hungry right now."

He watched them walk into the lunchroom, then turned to Baines, who looked as unkempt as ever. He was wearing a different shirt today, one with a gaudy yellow and orange design with a green T-shirt underneath it. Part of his shirt was tucked in, and part of it was hanging out. His hair was mussed as always, and a thick strand fell over one eyebrow.

"What's up, Charlie?"

"Well, in case you're interested, we found out the source of your E-mail."

"Who is it?"

"It's a little complicated. Can you come to the lab? I want Corey Ridder to explain it to you. She's the one who figured it out."

EIGHTEEN

Ridder was sitting in a cubicle in front of a glowing monitor and eating a peanut butter sandwich. She wore jeans and a baggy red sweatshirt that reached to her thighs. Her curly hair was tied to one side of her head, which gave her a slightly comical look.

"Here he is," Baines said. "I didn't tell him anything yet."

Ridder nudged her round eyeglasses further up the bridge of her nose as she slowly turned in her chair. "You're a football player, right?" Ridder asked without looking directly at him.

Will nodded, not greatly encouraged by her opening remark. No greeting, just a dumb question.

"Okay, three years ago, before any of us were here, there was a scandal about steroids being used by the football team." She still hadn't looked at him and he wondered why she was avoiding his gaze.

"I heard about it. What's that got to do with these messages I'm getting?"

Ridder raised her head, her large brown eyes finally

meeting his. He realized that even though she was usually in the lab when he was here, he'd never looked directly at her. There was something sensual in the flare of her nostrils and the curve of her mouth. At the same time there was a sense of depth about her.

"Everything," she said, softly.

She turned back to the computer and typed something on the keyboard. A list of names, each one followed by a series of numbers, appeared on the monitor. "Take a look."

Will recognized the names of players who'd been on the Aspen High football team while he was still in middle school.

"These are the guys who were involved. You getting this now?"

Will shook his head. "Not really. What are the numbers?"

"All right. These are all the E-mail codes that the players used. They thought they were real smart. They were buying and selling steroids via E-mail so they never had to talk about it."

She pointed to a name. "This guy handled the steroids." Her finger slid down the list. "And this one collected the money."

Will recognized the names of the two players who had been kicked off the team. But he didn't know anything about the electronic part of the transactions.

"A real team effort, you could say," Baines said. "See you guys later. I'm going to lunch."

A momentary look of panic crossed Ridder's face as she looked after Baines. For his own part, Will felt vaguely uneasy being left alone with Ridder, as if he might need a translator in order to understand what she said. Even if she was a computer wizard, she was still one of his classmates and he should have some things in common with her. "Corey?"

"Yeah?" She sounded wary.

"Is your name really Corey?"

"Corina. I hate it," she said without looking away from the monitor.

"So where did you get this information? I'm really impressed."

"Oh, that. I went into the administration's database and pulled it out."

"You can do that if you're a sysop?"

"Not really."

"You mean you hacked into it."

"That's one way of putting it."

"Isn't that dangerous?"

Ridder shrugged, unconcerned. "There are different degrees of danger. Say if you paid me a hundred dollars to change a grade from a C to an A, I'd say, yeah, that's on the high side. But just to take a quick look and get out without altering anything is on the lower scale."

Will peered at the screen again. "Corey, I'm sorry, but I still don't get what this has to do with the E-mail I've been getting."

"That's because you haven't realized yet how those football players were caught."

"So tell me."

Ridder closed the file and the screen went blank. Then she turned away from the computer and looked down the row of cubicles in each direction to make sure no one was within hearing distance. "That's the interesting part," she said, lowering her voice. "You see, when the principal who was here then got wind of what was going on, he told the sheriff, and detectives started arranging buys from the sheriff's office through E-mail."

"How did he do that without making the players suspicious?"

Ridder smiled. "They were allowed access to all active E-mail files and student codes. So they were not only able to find out who was making buys, but they also actually used players' codes to set up buys. That's how they caught the dealers."

"I wonder why I never heard about this E-mail stuff."

"Think about it. There weren't any trials, you know. The parents and their lawyers and money got involved and everything was settled behind closed doors. So, the methods that the sheriff's office used in their investigation were never revealed."

"You're saying that the sheriff's office was hooked into our computer system here?" Will was still confused about how this revelation connected with his problem.

"Not 'was,' is. They are hooked in." Ridder spun

around and began typing again. "Take a look at this."

She pointed at the screen and moved out of the way. Will leaned over for a closer look.

TO: PCSO
FROM: AHS
RE: 1996–97 LIST OF STUDENT
COMPUTER CODES

Below it was a long list of names followed by numbers. The school had sent the Pitkin County Sheriff's Office the E-mail codes of every student. "Are you telling me cops can read our E-mail?"

"Not only that, but they can create E-mail using your code. And someone did just that."

"A cop sent that E-mail to me? I can't believe this," Will said.

"It knocked me off my chair, too," Ridder said.

"But how do you know for sure that it's coming from the sheriff's office?"

Corey quickly explained how she'd found an extra digit in Will's private code and realized that it meant the messages had come from outside the school's computers. "That's when I went into the administration's system and found the list."

"But maybe someone else got hold of my code."

Ridder pushed her glasses up on her nose again and whispered. "No. I got proof. I snuck into the PCSO database."

"The sheriff's office? You're kidding."

"I've been there before, so it wasn't hard getting inside. I did a global search for your name and found all the letters that were sent to you."

Will was impressed, but he remembered that he'd told Detective Olsen about Fanz and the letters. "Maybe they just got copies of them."

"Yeah. That *was* a possibility. Except, I got lucky. I found a new one that Fanz had just written. It was in the PCSO system, but when I checked the school system, it wasn't here yet. It didn't arrive in your E-mail until five minutes after I'd read it in the PCSO system."

"Wow." Will's voice was barely audible.

"Yeah. Hope you didn't mind that I downloaded it."

Will's stomach knotted as he realized the implications of what Ridder was telling him. Not only was someone in the sheriff's office sending the E-mail but also that person was somehow involved in Myra's disappearance and probably her murder.

"What's the new message?"

Ridder reached down to the floor and picked up her purse. She found an envelope and took out a folded piece of paper. She handed it to Will.

So Burke's still got you fooled.
Too bad. Just too bad, Will.
Hate to see you go down
for his deadly little Chill.

Your Fanz

Will's hands were shaking. His head was spinning. He didn't know what to do, what to think. "Any idea who in the sheriff's office sent it?"

She shook her head. "I have no way of finding out who has access to the school's codes."

"Maybe I could ask Detective Olsen?"

"What if she's the one?"

He recalled seeing her last night with the same two men Burke had been talking to outside the Ute City Banque. "I hadn't thought of that."

"So who's Burke?" Ridder asked.

Just then Baines rushed into the room, out of breath. "Hey, Will, there's trouble on the way."

"What's going on?"

"A couple of sheriff's deputies opened up your locker a few minutes ago. The word is they scraped up traces of the Chill from the floor of the locker."

"That's impossible."

"Whether it is or not, they're looking for you right now."

Ridder grabbed Will's arm. "Go out the delivery door. You can get to it through the supply closet in back."

Will hesitated, surprised by Ridder's quick thinking, but uncertain what to do. "I don't know. I don't want to run."

"Someone's setting you up, Will."

She was right. He had to get away to think about what he should do next. He could always turn himself in later, maybe with his father at his side. "Okay, where's the door?"

"C'mon."

He followed her to the corner of the lab where she unlocked the supply closet. They hurried into a long room with steel shelves that were stacked with boxes of paper, printer ribbons, and pieces of equipment. At the far end, Ridder opened another door. To the right, ten feet away, were double doors painted red.

He turned back to Ridder. "Thanks a lot, Corey."

"I'm going with you."

"What?"

"You can't drive your car. They'll be looking for you. You can't drive mine, either. But I'll drive."

"Are you sure?"

She smiled. "Positive."

NINETEEN

Corey Ridder slid behind the wheel of her ten-year-old Mustang. She leaned over, popped open the lock, and Will dropped into the bucket seat. Seconds later, she backed out of the parking space. She was about to head for the exit to the street behind the school when a patrol car pulled into the lot.

"Go around the other way." Will slid down low in the seat.

Corey's heart pounded as she headed for the front exit. She stopped near the corner of the school and saw three patrol cars parked near the front entrance. "Uh-oh. Maybe I should turn around."

Will lifted his head and peered over the dashboard. "No, it'll look too suspicious. Just drive by like nothing is going on."

She held her breath as she drove past the empty patrol cars, and didn't exhale until she was on the street and driving away.

Just five minutes ago, the idea of going somewhere with Will had been a dream. She never expected it would really happen and certainly not this way. "Where should we go?"

"To my house. It's over on—"

"I know where you live." She shrugged, embarrassed. "I noticed the address when I was looking at the administration files." Then she quickly added, "What about the police? They might come looking for you there."

"I don't care. I've got to talk to my father." Will sat up again.

A few minutes later, she drove up to the three-story house on the edge of downtown. "It looks like my grandfather is out. His Land Rover's gone. Let me check the house."

Will raced to the door, unlocked it, and disappeared inside. Corey looked around feeling uneasy, expecting to see police cars at any moment. The front door slammed shut, and Will dashed back to the car.

"My dad must be out somewhere with my grandfather. He's got a car phone in the Land Rover, but it's turned off. Let's head over to my mother's shop."

As she drove away, Will touched Corey's arm. "Wait. I've got another idea. Go over to West End."

"What's there?"

"Tom Burke's place."

"Burke. That's the guy in the message. Do we really want to talk to him?"

"He's my mother's boyfriend, and I'm thinking that ol' Fanz just might be telling the truth."

Corey knew Will was caught in some sort of intricate web and she wondered if she was following him right into the heart of it. But oddly enough, she didn't care. She knew Will was innocent and she wasn't going to let him down.

"What are you going to say to him?"

"I don't know. I've got to think about it."

She nodded and forced herself to concentrate on pleasant thoughts to stay calm. She was with Will in her car, cruising around town. A dream come true. She tried to casually glance in the rearview mirror to see what her hair looked like. Probably a mess. Nothing she could do about it.

"This whole thing is about drugs," Will said, "a designer drug from Los Angeles. "But I don't understand why someone in the sheriff's office would be sending me these messages. What's the point?"

"Maybe someone's trying to get back at Burke for some reason."

Corey turned onto West End, and a block later Will pointed to a restored old Victorian house. "Do you know what you're going to say now?" she asked as she parked on the street.

"Nothing. His car's not here. I don't think he's home, but I remember my mother telling me about a spare key."

"You mean you want to go inside and look around?"

"Yeah. You can stay here."

"No, I'm going with you."

She zipped her jacket to her throat as they headed up the walkway. The sky was overcast, and after a couple of mild days, the temperature had plummeted and now hovered around freezing. They walked around the side of the old wood-frame house, then followed a flagstone path to a carriage house set back amid a stand of tall pines. Decades ago, the building had probably been used to store buggies and later cars until it was converted to a small apartment.

They stopped in front of the door and Will knocked. When there was no answer, he took a step back and looked puzzled.

"Where did your mother say the key was hidden?"

"That's the problem. I can't remember." He lifted the mat, but there was nothing beneath it. He tried to lift one of the flagstones near the door, but it wouldn't budge.

Corey, meanwhile, rose up on her toes and reached for the door ledge, but her fingertips just brushed the edge of the ledge. "Do you want me to give you a boost?" Will asked.

She hesitated. "Okay."

He wrapped his arms around her thighs and lifted her. She ran her hand along the ledge and knocked off something hard and flat that clattered to the ground.

Will eased her down and they both bent over and reached for the key, nearly bumping heads. She found it first and Will's fingers fell across the back of her hand. She looked up at him, their faces just inches apart.

"I've got it," she said in a soft voice. She handed it to him as they both stood up. Will looked embarrassed; she felt light-headed.

He put the key into the lock and opened the door. They stepped inside and Will quickly closed the door. The apartment was one large room with a high ceiling plus a bathroom. There was no kitchen, but a microwave oven and a toaster oven were kept on a shelf built along one wall. Next to it was an oak table with three chairs. There was no bed, but Corey guessed the couch folded out.

Will walked over to a rolltop desk and opened the top drawer. He rummaged through it, then moved on to another drawer. "Look at this!"

He held up a small plastic bag that was half full of a pale blue powder. Corey had never thought that anyone could look triumphant and disappointed at the same time, but that was exactly how she would describe Will's expression.

"What does it mean, Will?"

"I don't know. But I don't like it."

He stuffed the bag in his pocket and opened a file drawer. "Oh no."

"What is it?" she asked.

Will reached back behind a cluster of files and lifted out a large plastic freezer bag. It was stuffed with the blue powder.

"He must be dealing it," she said. "Do you think your mother knows about it?"

Will shook his head. "No, not my mother. I think he's got her fooled. Whenever she gets onto one of her antidrug kicks, Burke sits there and nods. But sometimes he sort of smirks. Now I know why."

"We better get out of here."

He shoved the bag back behind the files and closed the drawer. "I just want to look through a couple of more drawers."

Anxious to leave, Corey wandered over to a bookshelf near the door that was lined with videocassettes. She glanced at a few of the movie titles, then leaned closer as she noticed a slim black book wedged between *The Last Seduction* and *Speed*.

She felt guilty about snooping into someone else's belongings, but that was precisely why they'd come here. She opened the leather-bound booklet and paged through it.

"What is it?" Will asked.

"Just an address book. Names and telephone numbers. We better get out of here."

"Let me see it." Just as she handed the book to him, she saw movement in the yard. "Will, someone's coming up the walk."

There was no place to hide, no other doors. "What are we going to do?"

"Get down."

Will darted to the door and locked it. Then he dropped to his hands and knees and pointed to the kitchen table. There was a tablecloth on it that hung low over the sides. They crawled under it and huddled against the wall, their knees pulled tightly to their chests. Corey bit her lower lip and tried not to breathe.

She heard the key slip into the lock. The door opened and she saw a pair of boots and jeans from the knees down as someone, probably Burke, entered the apartment. He stopped by the table, his legs almost within reach. The room was completely quiet. It was as if he sensed their presence or something different about the room.

Then she heard a soft slap like a magazine or a stack of mail dropped on the table. The boots moved across the floor and into the bathroom. As the water was turned on in the sink, Will lifted a chair by the two front legs and carefully moved it out of the way. Then he crawled toward the door.

Corey didn't need any encouragement. She followed close behind. They stood up just as the water was turned off. Will put his hand on the doorknob. The toilet seat clattered down.

He eased the front door open and they sidled out. Corey darted through the grass, avoiding the flag-stones. She moved around the side of the main house and could see her Mustang parked across the street when she heard a car door slam shut. She slowed and Will caught up to her.

"Wait!" he hissed, touching her shoulder. He moved past her, edging along the side of the house to the front corner. A moment later, he turned back.

"Somebody's coming!"

They darted around the back of the house, pressed up against it. Corey heard footsteps, then saw a big, muscular guy with red curly hair walk by and continue on to Burke's apartment. She didn't see his face, but she thought he looked familiar.

"That's Claude Kirkpatrick," Will whispered. "What's he doing here?"

The sheriff's son, she thought. She'd seen him in the computer lab, and suddenly she started making connections, putting things together that hadn't made sense.

Claude tapped on the door, opened it, and disappeared inside. Corey was ready to get away, but Will motioned toward the house. "I'm going to see what I can find out." With that, he sprinted across the grass.

"Wonderful," Corey muttered. But she wasn't going to be left behind. She dashed across the yard and caught up with Will beneath a window. It was open a couple of inches and she could hear voices.

"I'm sorry, Tom. I'm sorry. It was that damn drug. I wasn't thinking clearly."

"You can blame everything on the drug, but the fact is you messed up big-time."

"If it wasn't for you and the drug, Myra would still be alive. The more I thought about what happened, the madder I got."

"Yeah, and you came close, very close, to sending us all to the slammer. Have they arrested Will yet?"

"That's what I wanted to talk to you about."

Will turned away and motioned Corey toward the street. She was more than happy to comply. As they crept away, she heard Burke cursing loudly. She was sure that Claude had just told him that Will had evaded the police.

Corey raced for the car and didn't look back until she was in the driver's seat.

"Let's go," Will said, slamming the passenger door shut. "I can't believe it. Here I thought Claude was my friend."

"It doesn't make sense, but he could be the one sending the messages," Corey said, pulling away from the curb. "He could've found his father's password and gotten into the system."

"But why?" Will asked. "He's in it with Burke."

Corey didn't have an answer.

"Let's go to my mother's place," Will said. He gave her directions to a clothing shop four blocks away.

They turned onto Hopkins Avenue and headed toward the center of downtown. A block later, Corey peered into the rearview mirror. She sucked in her breath. "Will, do you still have the little bag of the Chill with you?"

"Yeah."

"There's a city police car right behind us."

"Oh, great," Will muttered. "This is all I need. If I'm caught with this drug, no one's ever going to believe anything I say." He reached into his pocket for the crumpled bag. "Maybe I should throw it out the window."

"I don't think that's a good idea."

Will sunk lower in his seat. "Is he flashing his light?"

"Not yet. Oh, there. He turned."

She let out a sigh, relieved, as Will directed her into an alleyway behind the shop. "I'll go in the back door. Maybe you better go home now."

"No. I'll wait for you."

"Suit yourself." He started to open the door but changed his mind. He reached out, took her hand, and squeezed it. "Thanks, Corey."

Then he was gone and she barely heard him leave.

TWENTY

Will entered through the back door of the clothing shop and stopped next to a rack of ski parkas as his mother waited on a customer. Marion Connors looked over at him and smiled as she folded a sweatshirt that shouted ASPEN across the front. She slipped it into a bag and handed it to the woman.

"Will, glad you came by. I've got some good news for you," she said in a soft voice as she waited for the customer to leave.

"You do?" He walked up to the counter.

"I got a call from the lab. Your second urine test was negative for drugs."

"I bet someone tampered with the first one."

His mother frowned. "It could've just been a bad reading."

"Yeah, maybe. Mom, I've got to talk to you about Tom. I don't think you know everything about him."

"What do you mean?" Her voice tightened as she continued. "If this is about that silly computer message—"

"No, it's something else." He laid the plastic bag of the blue powder on the counter. "I found this in his desk drawer. I think it's the Chill. There was another bag, a big one, that was full of it—a couple of pounds at least."

Marion frowned as she looked at the bag. "What were you doing in his apartment?"

"I had to go and look. I got another E-mail message about him."

"What did it say?" Frowning, Marion picked up the plastic bag.

"That he's got something to do with this drug. I think I know who—"

"Will, there's something I've got to tell you. I've been putting it off and I—I didn't know why."

"What is it?" But he already knew, at least suspected what she was going to tell him.

"Tom wants me to marry him. But I told him I wanted to talk to you first."

Will didn't say anything. He couldn't say anything, didn't know what to say.

"If what you're telling me is true . . . all those trips to the West Coast. He must be doing more, a lot more than just trying out for roles."

"I'm sorry, Mom." He felt bad, but he was also relieved. Even if he were arrested, his mother now knew about Burke. But he still had plenty of unanswered questions.

The phone rang and Marion answered it on the first ring. "Aspen Apparel."

Her eyes narrowed as she listened. "That's right, Tom. Someone did break into your house and something was stolen. Your little bag of blue powder. I think you've got some explaining to do."

She slammed the phone down.

"I don't know if that was such a good idea, Mom. I'm getting kind of scared."

"Don't worry. I'm calling the police, too," she said, reaching for the phone.

Before he could say anything, the phone rang again. She snapped it up.

"What is it, Tom?" Her expression shifted, her features relaxing. "Oh, Dad. Yes, he's right here. Do you want to talk to him?"

She handed Will the phone and whispered, "Make it quick."

"Grandpa?"

"Will, listen. Do you remember that dream you had about John Wayne and that cave?"

"Yeah?"

"Well, that's been bothering me ever since you mentioned it the other night. I finally figured out why. The John Wayne Tunnel."

"What?"

"Up on the backside of the mountain is an old mine that I worked years ago. When John Wayne died, I dedicated it to his memory. I put up a plaque above the entrance with his name on it. It's a memorial to the Duke."

"I don't think I've ever seen it."

"Oh, yes you have, but you probably don't remember. I took you up there once when you were seven or eight."

A vague memory. Mining tunnels. John Wayne. His grandfather. It was all blurred together. "Do you think that's what I dreamed about?"

"Maybe. Dreams are funny things, Will. As your dad said, sometimes they show us things we don't realize we know. Anyhow, I think it's worth checking out. So does your dad. We were out for a drive and almost went up there, but decided to see if you wanted to come along. How about going up there right now? We've got a good three hours before dark."

There was so much to say and he didn't know where to begin, and he definitely wanted to talk to his father. "That's fine. I'll be waiting."

"What's going on?" Marion asked after Will hung up.

"Grandpa's got an idea about where Myra's body might be. We're going to take a look. Dad's going, too. They'll pick me up out front."

She nodded. "Maybe it's better that you're not around for a while. Things could get a little messy after I call Detective Olsen."

"Don't call Olsen, Mom. Not yet," Will said, heading toward the back door.

"Why not?"

"I think she might be involved. I'll explain later. I've got a friend waiting for me."

"Wait a minute. What friend?"

"She's a sysop from the computer lab."

"A sysop, what's that?"

"Later, Mom."

"Be careful, Will."

"You too."

He hurried out the door before his mother could ask what she was doing in the alley.

"Sorry it took so long," he said as he slid into the seat next to Corey.

She smiled and looked relieved. "I was getting worried that something happened."

"My father and grandfather are going to take me up the mountain to an old mine shaft. They think it might be where Myra was taken."

"I want to go with you."

"I don't know. It could be dangerous."

"Will, if I didn't help you get out of the lab, you'd be in jail right now."

He was surprised at how adamant she sounded. "Okay. Go around the front and find a parking spot."

As they waited for his grandfather's Land Rover to arrive, Will took out the address book from his back pocket and paged through it. There were a few full names, like Bill Wharton, Jerry's father, but most were first names and initials for the last name or just initials. Among them were G. T. and Henry D. He wondered if G. T. was George Thomas, Aaron's father, and Henry D. was Paige Davis's father. Both were among Burke's movie industry pals. G. T.'s phone number wasn't the same as Aaron's, but that wasn't surprising. Most of his friends had their own phone lines.

"That's interesting," he said as his finger stopped on an unusual name.

"What is it?" Corey asked.

"P-R-O period T-E-C. PRO.TEC, that's the name, and I know this phone number. It's the Kirkpatricks'."

"PRO.TEC. Could that be short for 'protection'?" Corey wondered.

"Or protector," Will said. "I guess that must be Claude."

"Unless it's the sheriff himself. Maybe he's protecting Burke in his drug dealings."

"If the sheriff is involved, this thing is really big." Will closed the address book and looked around. "Hurry up, Grandpa."

Sheriff's deputies were bound to arrive at his mother's shop anytime looking for him. They would spot two kids sitting in a car and they'd nab him.

But it wasn't the police or his grandfather who showed up first. Aaron Thomas was walking down the sidewalk, headed in their direction. Will was about to slide down in the seat when Thomas made eye contact. He grinned, played an air guitar, then made a passing motion with his hand.

"Oh, no," Will moaned.

Thomas's square jaw, blue eyes, and blond hair

filled the window. He tapped on the glass, motioning Will to roll it down.

"Hi, Aaron."

"Hey, you're hot, man. You are hot. The sheriff's department has a friggin' posse out lookin' for you."

He peered past Will at Corey, snapped his fingers and pointed at her. "I know you." He shook his head. "You're full of surprises, Will. Who're you guys, Bonnie and Clyde? What's going on?"

"It's kind of hard to explain right now."

"Will!" Corey tapped him on the shoulder. The Land Rover had pulled up next to the Mustang.

Without another word, Will and Corey jumped out and dashed around the Mustang. Will opened the back door of his grandfather's car for Corey, then slid in after her.

"Let's go, Grandpa. Hi, Dad."

He glanced back at Aaron, who looked baffled but managed to recover in time to make a quick passing motion with his hand. His way of saying "Go for it."

"Who do we have with us, Will?" Ed Connors asked, peering into the rearview mirror as he drove away.

"This is Corey Ridder. If it wasn't for her, I wouldn't be here right now," Will said and began explaining everything that had happened this afternoon.

As soon as Pete Lansa heard that Will was wanted, he told Connors to stop. He turned in his seat as the Land Rover eased off the road. His face was expressionless, his dark eyes staring at Will from above his high cheekbones.

"Will, I believe you if you say that someone planted that drug in your locker. Even if you were involved with drugs, you're too smart to leave any in your locker."

"So why are we stopping, Dad?"

"Because I don't believe in running from the police. We've got to take you to the station."

"Wait," Corey said. "You don't know everything yet."

She quickly told Lansa about their visit to Tom Burke's apartment, about the drugs, the notebook, and the possible identification of PRO.TEC.

Connors cursed under his breath when she mentioned Burke. "I should've known he wasn't any good. He's too slick, but Marion kept saying I didn't like him because he is an actor."

"You're certain that's Kirkpatrick's home phone number?" Lansa asked, looking at the page in the address book.

Will nodded. "It's the old number I used to call before Claude got his own line last year."

"I want to try calling it, anyhow," Lansa said. "Can you find a phone booth, Ed?"

"Who needs a phone booth?" Connors pulled out his cellular phone from a compartment in his car door and turned it on. "What's the number?" He punched it and held the phone far enough from his ear so that Will could hear the ringing. A recorded voice answered and identified the Kirkpatrick residence.

Connors pushed the "end" button on the back of the cell phone.

"That's it, all right," Connors said. "But we don't know if the protector is the sheriff or his son."

"It could be both of them," Corey said. "The sheriff could be protecting his son."

Lansa nodded. "I don't want you in Kirkpatrick's jail, Will. We'll drive to Denver. I've got an old friend there, who's now the assistant chief of police. We'll give him the notebook."

"What about the mine?" Will asked.

Lansa hesitated.

"We've got to make a run up there first," Connors said. "It just dawned on me."

"What did?" Lansa asked.

"Burke owns the claim on the John Wayne Tunnel."

"He's a miner?" Lansa asked, doubtfully.

"Last winter Burke started talking about how he wanted to try his hand at mining for silver. He said he had a couple of friends who were interested in working with him. I thought it was just talk, but he kept on about it. So this past spring I made a deal with him on one of my claims that hasn't been worked for twenty years."

Will remembered Burke and his grandfather talking about mining. At the time, Will thought it was just an effort by Burke to get on his grandfather's good side. But he also knew his grandfather had sold a couple other mining claims and that was probably how Burke had gotten the idea.

"Have you been up there since then?" Will asked.

"Just once. Late May, I think it was. No one was around, but there'd been a lot of digging. Lately though, Burke hasn't said a word about the mine."

"Okay," Lansa said. "Let's go up there and take a quick look around."

TWENTY-ONE

They turned off the highway and followed a dirt road that switched back and forth up the mountain. Soon patches of wet snow speckled the landscape, and the higher they went, the larger the patches became until a continuous, gleaming mass of white covered the ground and road. Large heavy flakes fluttered from the gray sky, adding to the recent accumulation.

They rounded a bend and the edge of the road fell away. Will looked out over the spidery thicket of barren aspen trees outlined against a field of snow and wondered what they would find at the mine.

With their course of action firmly in mind, Will relaxed a bit and laughed as he told Lansa and Connors how he and Corey must have surprised Aaron Thomas when he saw them suddenly switch vehicles and drive away without saying another word to him.

But his father didn't join in Will's laughter. "That's too bad. By now the sheriff probably knows you're in this vehicle. It's going to be harder to get away."

"Do you think Aaron would tell anyone?" Corey asked.

"I don't know," Will said, reassessing the situation.

The scenery was obscured by a black mound of tailings, partially glazed with fresh snow. Connors nodded toward it. "You see that, Corey? A lot of people just think these tailing piles are an eyesore. But for miners like me they represent a lot of hard work by honest people. I'm proud of them."

Corey peered out the window at the tailings and said she'd like to know more about Aspen's mining history. "I'd be glad to tell you all about it sometime, young lady."

Will was sympathetic to his grandfather's views, but he also knew that the tailing piles were more than just an eyesore. They were also a source of water pollution that had affected Aspen and other former mining communities. As his father once said: You can't continually take from the earth without eventually paying a price.

"Okay, we're not far now," Connors said. "Just another quarter mile or so. Then we'll find out if Will's dream was telling us something important."

The dirt road widened, and Connors eased the car over to the side. As they got out, Lansa stared down at the tire tracks covered by the fresh snow. "There's been activity here recently. Several vehicles. A couple of them were here within the last few hours."

Will looked at the barely perceptible maze of tracks. He would've never noticed them, and he certainly couldn't put them in any sort of time frame, except that they were made before the latest snowfall.

"This way," Connors said and led the way along a

snow-covered trail. Even though his grandfather was close to seventy, he was wiry and healthy and moved with surprising agility across the rugged landscape.

Will zipped his jacket against the late afternoon chill. The crisp air still held the pungent scent of decaying leaves.

He glanced back at Corey, who was walking a few feet behind him. She ran a hand through her curly hair, brushing the snowflakes away, and smiled back self-consciously.

"You see, Burke and his buddies were working up here," Connors said as he walked around a heap of rubble. A shovel was jammed into the top of the mound like a tilting flagpole. "This is all from last spring."

On the far side of the mound were narrow gauge rail tracks that led into the mountain. Above the entrance to the tunnel, imbedded in the earth, was a wooden plaque. Connors raised up on his toes and wiped the snow away. The plaque read THE JOHN WAYNE TUNNEL. The letters were carved in a hard wood that had weathered well over the years.

"I wanted to use silver for the plaque, but I know damn well somebody would've come along and stolen it before too long," Connors said.

Will ducked into the tunnel and was greeted by a dank odor of earth. The tunnel was narrow and just high enough for him to stand up. A few yards inside, a rust-colored iron cart rested on the tracks. The handle of another shovel was sticking out of the top. The tracks continued several more yards, then disappeared under a heavy wooden round-top door. A thick padlock secured it shut.

Connors shined a flashlight on it. "That door and lock are new. I wonder what he's got in there."

"So do I," Lansa said.

Will looked inside the cart. There was something lying on the bottom. It was too dark to see what it was. "Gramps, can you shine your flashlight in here?"

The beam struck the floor of the cart, and Will saw that it was just a coil of rope. Then the beam momentarily played across another object. "What was that?" Will asked.

Connors aimed the flashlight into the corner.

"That's Myra's shoe. I'm sure of it. She was wearing brown loafers the night she disappeared," Will said.

Lansa took the flashlight and leaned over the cart. "There're dark stains on the cart. It might be blood."

"I bet the body's inside," Corey said. "They put it in the cart first, then moved it."

"That's what I was just thinking," Connors said.

"You've got your gun with you, don't you, Dad? Why don't you shoot the lock."

Lansa walked over to the door. "That only works in the movies, Will. I've got a .38, not a cannon. That's a heavy lock."

"I've got a crowbar and a hammer in the Land Rover," Connors said.

"I'll go get them." Will jogged out of the tunnel and down the trail.

TWENTY-TWO

Corey had wanted to go back with Will, just to be alone with him again. To find out what he was thinking. To listen to him talk. But he didn't invite her, and she didn't want to seem too eager to tag along. Besides, this was a serious matter, not an outing in the woods, and she had a bad feeling about this place. The sooner they left, the better.

Will's father and grandfather were looking around outside, but she had decided to stay in the tunnel. She took the lock in her hand, felt its weight and shape. Locks were like people. They had both outer and inner strength. Some of the ones that appeared big and strong were weak inside, and vice versa. She realized immediately that she was looking at one of the former types.

She smiled as she reached into the untamed thicket on her head and pulled a bobby pin from just above her ear. It wasn't doing much good anyhow. In fact, most of her attempts at controlling her hair were more wishful thinking than anything else.

She quickly worked the pin into the lock and moved it around with the assurance of an expert locksmith. She'd always had a knack for breaking into things, whether it was computer systems or locks with no keys. Usually it was easier for her to finesse her way in rather than use brute strength. For example, she preferred guessing at secret passwords rather than running mathematical programs that would automatically try hundreds of thousands or even millions of word or number combinations. With locks, she preferred a pin or a paper clip over a sledgehammer.

She closed her eyes as she worked, feeling her way. Finally, she pushed and twisted and the lock popped open. "Nothing to it," she said aloud.

She removed the lock from the hasp, and the door creaked open several inches. She hesitated, thinking that she should wait for the others, but then impulsively she leaned against the door. Faint light filtered through the doorway, and she knew immediately that this was no ordinary mine. It was no mine at all.

"Corey!"

She spun around. "Oh, you scared me."

Connors stood behind her. "What the hell! You got the door open?"

She immediately felt wary. She'd learned long ago that adults usually didn't appreciate being upstaged, especially by a black girl. "I picked the lock," she said with a shrug.

"Hey, that's great. You should've said something

before Will left. So what do we got inside?"

She let him go in first with his flashlight. She liked Will's grandfather, even though he seemed sort of gruff. Will's father was more like Will, quiet and thoughtful. Except that he was quieter than Will.

"What in the world!" Connors exclaimed. "I don't believe what I'm seeing."

TWENTY-THREE

Will hurried back to the tunnel, a ten-pound sledge-hammer in one hand and a crowbar in the other. But he stopped short when he saw someone standing at one side of the trail. A hole in the overcast sky had opened and a ray of light filtered through the trees, forming a halo effect around the figure. For a moment, Will thought he saw feathers streaming out from the top of the man's head.

"Dad? Is that you?"

Without responding, the man turned and walked into the woods. Will followed him, but when he reached the top of a rise, the man was no longer in sight. He looked for tracks in the snow, but didn't see any. The forest wasn't particularly dense here and with no leaves on the trees, he could easily see a couple of hundred yards. But nothing moved. There was no one out there.

Will headed back to the trail, wondering if he'd really seen the man. A low, shrill whistle suddenly raised the hair on the back of his neck. He looked over his shoulder and saw the man standing on the rise that Will had just vacated.

This time he saw him clearly and recognized him. It was the same beaming face he'd seen last summer at the Spring of Shadows, at the game, and in his dreams. Masau.

"Will?"

He turned at the sound of his father's voice. "What are you doing over there?"

He glanced back to the rise, but the man was gone. He hurried over to his father. "Dad, I saw him again. Masau was standing right up there."

His father nodded, looking toward the direction Will was pointing. He didn't question him as his grandfather would have done, nor did he seem surprised.

Will felt more awed than disturbed or frightened by what he'd just seen. In fact, this time he wasn't frightened at all. Maybe his father's presence and the reassurances he'd already given him about his mystical experiences were bolstering his confidence.

"Masau is guiding you, but he's not necessarily protecting you," Lansa said.

"What do you mean?"

"It means we have to hurry."

They trotted back to the tunnel without saying any more about Masau, but Will felt that his father was holding something back. He entered the tunnel right behind his father and waited for him to move past the mining cart.

Lansa held up a hand for him to be quiet, then

pointed at the door. The lock lay on the ground and the door was ajar. He poked his head through the door, and Will looked over his shoulder. The door creaked open a few more inches. At first, all he could see was a flashlight beam that crossed the wall, then shone in his eyes. He held up a hand to block the light.

"Pete, Will, c'mon in here," Connors said. "You've got to see this."

"How did you get the lock open?" Will asked as he and his father stepped inside.

"Our young lady friend here happens to be handy with a hairpin."

Will looked over at Corey, but his attention was immediately distracted as Connors moved the light around the room.

The beam illuminated a room that was about twenty by twenty with a concrete floor and finished walls and ceiling. A long counter dominated the center of the room and it was covered with beakers, racks of test tubes, Bunsen burners, and other lab equipment. Nearby was a metal storage rack stocked with canisters marked with chemical names.

"It looks like a chemistry lab," Will said.

"That's exactly what it is," Corey said, picking up a beaker. "This must be where that drug is made."

"Burke isn't a chemist, though," Will said.

"You can bet one of his partners is," Connors said. "They probably figured they'd found the perfect spot for a drug lab."

"But there's no sign of Myra here," Will said.

"Will, I found what looks like a grave not a hundred feet from the entrance," Lansa said.

"Where? I want to see it." Will headed toward the door. On his way out of the tunnel, he grabbed the shovel that was in the mining cart.

Lansa led the way over to what appeared to be a grave. To Will's surprise, the spot wasn't particularly well hidden. Anyone walking this way from the entrance of the mine could see the overturned soil. He wondered about that and why the body would be buried so close to a place that the killer probably wanted to keep secret.

"If Myra was buried here, she hasn't been here long," Lansa said.

"Why do you say that?" Connors asked.

"This soil was dug up earlier today. There were three people here and they made no effort to cover their shoe prints. Two men, one woman. She wore hiking boots. The men wore sneakers."

"How can you see that through the snow?" Corey asked.

He pointed to a barren spot to one side. "I blew the snow away over there."

"I've got to see if the body's here." Will plunged the shovel into the dirt.

"Will, you don't want to do that," Connors said. "Besides, you're messing up the evidence."

"I don't think you're going to find a body."

"What do you mean, Dad? This is a grave, isn't it?"

When Lansa didn't answer, Will quickly scooped several more shovelfuls of the loose dirt. Three feet down and he hit solid ground. He stabbed the shovel at the loose dirt nearby and again struck hard ground.

"I don't get it. How did you know there wasn't a body here?"

"Because there were other tracks here, too, that were from a few days ago. I think it was only one person. The body was probably buried here, but then it was dug up by the three others."

"You amaze me," Connors said. "But what does this mean?"

"It could mean the killer got scared and moved the body. But why would he involve two more people?"

"And why would he bury the body here in the first place?" Corey asked. "It's so close to the tunnel."

"Good point," Lansa said. "I don't think we're going to find any more answers here right now. We better be on our way."

As they headed to the Land Rover, Will lagged behind. Something told him to stop and look back. He slowly turned his head and saw Masau standing on the grave, his face haggard and bloody. Will couldn't move. His heart pounded and he heard Masau's voice inside his head: *Here comes the murderer.*

"Will!" Connors yelled. "Let's move it."

He tore his gaze away, then hurried to catch up to the others. He didn't know whether he should say anything or not. But then he glimpsed what the others had already seen. A four-wheel-drive police vehicle was coming up the winding mountain road.

They rushed into the Land Rover, and Connors gunned the engine and pulled away, bouncing over the rugged dirt road. "I hate the idea of running from cops, but we've got no choice. That might be Kirkpatrick."

"Bad cops can be more dangerous than hardened criminals," Lansa said. "They've got the power, or the appearance of it, on their side."

"You've got that right." Connors glanced into the rearview mirror. "I think we got away before they saw us."

But how were they going to get to Denver without being stopped? Will wondered. If Kirkpatrick didn't already have an all-points bulletin out for the Land Rover, it wouldn't be long before he figured out Will was with his grandfather. Besides, they couldn't leave right away since they had to drop off Corey before they left town.

"Do you know how to get to the highway this way?" Lansa asked.

"Of course. I know these roads like the back—"

Connors slammed on the brakes and cursed under his breath. Two pickups were blocking the road. He stopped a hundred feet short of the trucks.

"Maybe they just stopped to look at something," Corey said hopefully.

"I don't think so," Will said as he saw Detective Olsen step out and raise her gun.

Two men, both armed, stepped out from either side of the road and aimed their weapons at the Land Rover. They wore black jeans and leather jackets. One had a ponytail, the other a thick black beard and curly hair. They were the same pair Will had seen with Burke outside the Ute City Banque, and later with Olsen.

"Get out of the car," Olsen yelled. "Hands in the air."

"Do what she says," Lansa said, and they all stepped out of the vehicle.

"Put your hands down on the hood," Olsen ordered as she moved closer.

The two men ran their hands down Will's, Lansa's, and Connors's sides and legs and found Lansa's .38. Olsen searched Corey, who stood next to Will in stunned silence.

"What were you doing at the mine?" Olsen asked.

"We were looking for John Wayne," Connors said. "But we found a drug factory instead. You know that, though, don't you, Detective?"

"Yes, we do."

Will felt dazed, light-headed. Olsen and Kirkpatrick must be involved with Burke in the drug scheme.

An engine growled as the police vehicle they'd seen coming up the mountain stopped behind the Land Rover. Sheriff Kirkpatrick got out and touched his hand to his holstered weapon.

"Just keep your hands on the hood," Olsen

murmured. "Everything will be okay."

"Good work, Laura," Kirkpatrick said. "Did you follow them up here?"

"No, we were already here."

Will glanced over his shoulder and saw Kirkpatrick frown. "I thought you were off today."

Olsen didn't answer.

Kirkpatrick looked at the two men. "Who're your helpers?"

"They're DEA agents, Bower. You're under arrest. We've been staking out the mine. We've got videotape of you and Tom Burke going in and out of it."

"I was setting him up," Kirkpatrick said.

"Tell it to the judge," she said and handcuffed him as Ponytail disarmed him.

Will was stunned by the abrupt turnabout. He wasn't the only one.

"I don't believe this," Kirkpatrick said.

"Yeah, there goes the election, Bower," Olsen said. "Sorry about that."

A car door slammed. Claude, followed by Paige Davis, walked over from the police vehicle. "What's going on here?" Claude asked.

"Funny you should ask," Olsen said. "You're under arrest for murder."

Will felt elated and sickened at the same time. Olsen knew that he was innocent. But his former best friend was a killer. He realized Olsen must have been acting when she and the DEA agents had confronted

Will and the others. It was just a setup to catch the Kirkpatricks.

"What are you talking about?" Claude's voice was nearly a screech. "I didn't kill anyone."

"We videotaped you yesterday when you dug the grave, then buried the body after you carried it out of the mine," Ponytail said. "We dug it up today when we brought Detective Olsen up here."

"Who are you guys? I thought—"

"Shut up!" Black Beard snapped.

"I didn't kill her," Claude blubbered. "Paige did it. She was on the drug. I stole Will's knife out of his Jeep to make it look like it was him."

"You made me kill her," Paige screamed. "You were afraid she was going to turn in the whole operation. She knew too much."

"Shut your mouth!" the sheriff yelled. "Both of you! Don't say another word. It's not what you think."

Olsen snapped handcuffs on Claude and Paige. "What is it then, Bower? She's said plenty already."

Suddenly, another vehicle appeared—a dark green Ford Explorer. It skidded to a stop just behind the police car, and Tom Burke stepped out.

"Well, now the real fun begins," Ponytail said with a laugh.

TWENTY-FOUR

Burke's gaze took in everything and everyone. He didn't seem at all surprised or concerned. If he thought he was going to talk himself out of this mess, it was going to take an Oscar-winning performance.

"Put your hands on the vehicle," Olsen snapped. "You're under arrest."

Burke gave her an amused look. He glanced at the two DEA agents and smiled. Black Beard put his gun to Olsen's head. "Sorry, Laura."

Ponytail reached for the astonished detective's gun.

"What's going on?" she asked.

"Who are you guys?" Connors looked bewildered.

Burke spun around. He held a snub-nosed .38 in his palm. "On the ground, Ed. All of you." He motioned toward Lansa, Will, and Corey. "Hands behind your heads."

Burke turned back to Olsen. "Don't worry, these guys really are DEA agents. It's just that they have some outside interests." He nodded toward Black

Beard. "Charles here is our chemist. That came in very handy for the lab work."

"The best thing you can do right now is give up," Olsen said in a surprisingly calm voice.

Burke laughed. "I admit it was getting a little hot with that nasty murder. Claude here got messed up on the drug and almost ruined everything. He tried to get back at me by sticking the body in the mining cart and sending a bunch of E-mail crap to Will. But that's over now. We've got our goods out of town and now it's time to blow this place."

He looked at his partners and grinned. "And I mean blow it."

"Get these things off me," Kirkpatrick said, shaking his wrists.

Burke held out his hand to Olsen. "The keys, please. It's time for musical handcuffs."

Black Beard pushed his 9-mm pistol to Olsen's forehead. She reached into her jacket and handed Burke the keys.

Will saw a look of intense concentration on his father's face. His body was tensed as if he were ready to act.

"First, the sheriff." He freed Kirkpatrick and handed him the cuffs and keys. "I'll let you do the honors. You've got more experience in these matters."

"Watch out!" Kirkpatrick yelled.

Lansa leaped to his feet and wrapped an arm around Burke's neck and grabbed his hand. He dragged him back, away from the others, as he struggled for the gun. Will bolted forward and rammed his head into the sheriff's gut, knocking him into Ponytail. Claude hurtled into Lansa, catching him behind the knees. Burke fell on top of Lansa and his gun fired.

Will looked up to see Paige falling to the ground, Corey racing into the woods, and Burke striking his father's head with the butt of his gun. Will started to crawl, but Kirkpatrick lunged and grabbed his legs. Ponytail rushed over and pressed his gun against Will's cheek.

A few feet in front of Will, Paige lay on her back, breathing hard. Blood covered her chest. Her eyes were open wide. Then she was still.

"No!" Claude yelled. He rushed over and dropped to his knees. "Paige, no!"

Will looked away. Black Beard was holding Olsen with an arm locked around her neck. But Corey, where was Corey?

"Paige is dead!" Claude shouted. "No!"

Will looked up just in time to see the sheriff's boot an instant before it struck him in the center of the forehead.

TWENTY-FIVE

She didn't want to leave Will behind, but there was nothing else Corey could do. She'd waited for her chance and as soon as Will had tackled the sheriff, she'd bolted for the woods. She didn't know what happened to Will or his father, but she had to get help.

She ran blindly in a zigzag path, going uphill, then down, dodging trees as she went. She didn't know where she was or which way to go. She finally stopped and put her hands on her knees, gasping for air. Her head was spinning.

She was about to start off again when she heard the crunch of snow, someone following her footprints. She couldn't tell how far away the sounds were or the exact direction they were coming from.

But they were definitely closer, coming closer.

Her heart pounding in her ears, she dashed away from the sound, running uphill through an area almost devoid of snow, then downhill, keeping to forested areas and away from snow-covered fields. When she stopped again, she didn't move for a full minute and she didn't hear any sounds of footsteps.

The afternoon was fading away into a murky gray. Soon it would be dusk, then dark. She'd gotten away, she thought, but she was lost. She wasn't so much afraid for herself now as she was concerned about Will and the others. She couldn't help them, couldn't do a thing, unless she quickly found her way out of the forest.

For all she knew, she might be wandering in a circle and wind up back by the mine. She calmed herself, gathered her thoughts, and realized that she must go down the mountain. Eventually, she would find a road. She plunged down a steep incline, skidding, grabbing tree trunks to slow her descent. At the bottom of the ravine, she stopped to catch her breath, then continued on.

Ten minutes later, she came to a rutted trail. She followed it down to a dirt road. *It must be the same one they'd been driving on,* she thought. She jogged in the downhill direction, keeping to the side of the road. Every so often she looked back over her shoulder. If a vehicle appeared, she'd be tempted to wave it down. At the same time, she knew there was a good chance it would be the sheriff, Burke, or the others. There was no doubt in her mind that they were looking for her.

The road curved and the forest fell away. Across the field in front of her was a log cabin. A thin stream of smoke twisted from a chimney, and there was a light in the window. She took one more look behind her, then dashed through the field.

As she neared the cabin, her hopes plummeted. There was no vehicle in sight and the place looked primitive. An old-fashioned well stood fifty feet from the cabin, and there was an outhouse behind it. The flickering light suggested the place was illuminated by a lantern.

She slowed to a walk just as a woman in a long denim skirt and a white blouse stepped out with a bucket and headed toward the well. The woman spotted her and stopped. Corey felt as if she'd just gone back a hundred years. No running water and no electricity. And probably no help.

"Are you okay?" the woman asked. She set the pail down and pushed her long brown hair over her shoulder.

Corey blurted her story, pointing to the road in the direction of the mine. She kept it simple. She and her friends had stumbled upon a drug factory and drug dealers. Guns. Fighting. Shooting. And she'd escaped. She needed help. Inside the cabin a baby began to cry and the woman, who said her name was Irene, motioned for Corey to follow her. "Max is in town. I don't have any transportation. Is there someone you can call?"

"You have a telephone?"

"Sure do." The woman scooped up the baby from a crib, walked over to the kitchen counter, and picked up a cellular phone not much larger than her palm. "I wouldn't be up here without one. I'll tell you that."

Corey took the phone and tried to think who she

should call. Her parents were both on the road. Her mother wouldn't be home until tomorrow afternoon. She remembered the name of Will's mother's shop: Aspen Apparel. She dialed information and got the number.

"You're calling a clothing store?" Irene asked as Corey punched the number.

"I can't call the police; they're part of the drug ring." A woman's voice answered with the name of the shop. "Mrs. Lansa?"

There was a pause. "Connors. This is Marion Connors. Are you calling about Will? What's going on?"

Of course, she had a different last name. "Yes, I'm sorry. Ms. Connors, Will needs your help badly."

Corey quickly explained what happened.

"Okay, I'll get help."

"You don't understand. There's no time. You have to leave right now. Do you have a gun?"

"Yes."

"Bring it and hurry! Please!"

Before she hung up, Corey handed the phone to Irene who explained how to reach the cabin.

"She said she's on her way," Irene said as she hung up. "With any luck, she should be here in half an hour. But it's slow going on these slippery roads at night. How about a cup of coffee?"

Corey shook her head. "I just hope she gets here in time."

Just then headlights beamed into the window.

Irene went to the door. She spun around. "It's a police car. Maybe you better . . ."

But Corey was already out the back door, running as fast as she could through the growing darkness, passing the outhouse, and dashing for the forest.

TWENTY-SIX

Will's vision was blurred, his head pounded. It was dark and stuffy. There were fuzzy figures moving around and voices he couldn't quite understand. He was lying on a cool, damp floor. A rope was tied around his feet and his wrists; his arms were behind his back. *The drug lab*, he thought, as he recalled everything that had happened before he'd been knocked out.

In the center of the room, a light glowed on the lab counter where Burke and the two DEA agents were busy at work. His father was lying to Will's left next to Detective Olsen. Their wrists were cuffed in front of them and their feet were tied with rope. His grandfather lay on his right, bound the same way.

Corey had gotten away, he thought. The sheriff and Claude were probably hunting for her. They couldn't let her escape. He realized that Burke and the others couldn't allow any of them to survive and tell their story.

He felt heavy, as if he'd been drugged. He fought off the dizzying sensation that was trying to pull him back into a deep sleep.

He moved his hands, testing the rope, stretching it. He had to get loose, but his vision was blurring. He was drifting, losing consciousness again. His eyes closed, and he heard a voice in his head.

You can dream your way out. Dream.

Flickering firelight. He was with the initiates in the kiva again. It was happening all over. Near the fire pit, a robed man was talking to them and pointing up through the ladder hole. He was speaking Hopi, and again Will could understand him.

Suddenly, the old priest covered the fire pit with a flat rock so that only a faint glow filtered into the kiva. The men in robes descended the ladder. On each of their foreheads was a large four-pointed white star.

Among them was Masau, his head bald and painted gray.

He moved to one side of the other men who were humming and hissing. A white-robed figure emerged and said, "I am the beginning; I am the end."

It was all the same as before, but Will was only vaguely aware that the scene was familiar. The sounds grew louder, and the men were stomping one way, then the other. Suddenly, the flat rock was pushed over the entire fire pit and darkness swallowed the kiva. Amid the shouts and chaos, Will saw Masau standing directly in front of him and motioning to the ladder hole overhead.

Then it was Myra, not Masau. She was smiling at him and, like Masau, pointing to the hole overhead. *That's the way out, Will. That's the way. Hurry.*

Will's body jerked and he blinked open his eyes. He tried to sit up. His head throbbed from the blow; he was confused by what he'd just experienced. The kiva had seemed just as real as the mine.

"Will, are you okay?" his grandfather asked in a raspy voice.

He looked over at him and Olsen, and nodded.

Burke and the two others were gone. How long had he slept?

"They left a bomb," his father said from his other side. "Burke said we've got half an hour. Now it's about twenty-five minutes."

"Special effects," Connors said. "Burke's a bomb expert. That's what his daddy taught him."

"Can you get your hands loose?" Olsen asked Will.

"What good will it do?" Connors said. "You heard what Burke said. "The door's rigged. If we open the door, the bomb goes off."

"Maybe we can disarm it," Lansa said.

Will recalled his dream. *That's the way out,* Myra had said. He looked up at the paneled ceiling. Maybe there was another way out, an escape hatch they'd built in the event of trouble.

He jerked his arms apart, stretching, then twisting the rope. He wriggled his hands, moved them back and forth, and tried to slip the rope over his wrists. But it wasn't quite loose enough.

"I've got a knife on my key chain," Connors said. "It's in my jacket pocket. See if you can get it out."

Will rolled over and worked himself next to his grandfather, then stretched his hand into Connors's pocket. He felt the key chain, but couldn't reach it. He edged closer, tried again, but Connors moved. On the third try, his index finger hooked over the chain.

"I got it!"

He worked open the blade with his fingers, then passed it to his grandfather who began slicing away at the rope binding Will's wrists. After a couple of minutes, Lansa took over, then Olsen. The detective had taken about a dozen slices when Will jerked his wrists and the rope snapped. Once his hands were free, he quickly untied the rope from his ankles. Then he went to work on the rope tied around his grandfather's legs.

When he finally got the knot undone, he handed the knife to his grandfather. "See if you can get their legs free."

"What are you going to do?" his father asked.

"I think there might be another way out of here, Dad."

He moved over to the counter and saw a box on the floor in front of the lab counter. Inside it was a red metal one-gallon gasoline can, a tangle of wires, and a timer that showed nineteen minutes were left. He glanced over at the door and saw a small plastic box attached to it. Probably a remote detonator.

He climbed up onto the counter and picked up the battery-powered lamp that had been left behind. With his other hand, he reached up to the ceiling and lifted one of the plastic panels. The lamp's glow revealed an eighteen-inch crawl space separating the ceiling from the rock roof. He raised the lamp higher. To his left, a rectangular piece of wood was imbedded in the ceiling. A cord hung down from it.

"What do you see?" Connors asked.

"A trap door, I think." He lowered the panel, then tiptoed through the hodgepodge of glassware and burners on the counter.

Will was about to remove another panel, when his foot knocked over a beaker. It rolled toward the edge of the counter. He reached down and caught it before it fell. Directly below was the bomb. No telling what would've happened if the beaker had fallen on it.

He lifted the panel, pushed it aside, and pulled on the cord. The rectangle of plywood creaked down on its hinges. Attached to the inside of it was a ladder, which he unfolded. The bottom of it reached the top of the counter.

"Does it lead outside, Will?" his father called to him.

"I can't tell." He held up the light, stepped onto the ladder. He could see a tunnel that was slightly wider than his shoulders. It rose at a steep angle. *The dream,* he thought. It was like the ladder hole in the top of the kiva. He knew he'd find a way out. But he didn't think the others would be able to maneuver through the tunnel with their hands bound.

"If you get out, run as fast as you can," Lansa called to him. "We're stuck here, but you can make it. You hear me."

Connors was busy sawing at the rope on Olsen's ankles.

"I don't want to leave you," Will said. "We've still got time."

Before his father started to argue, Will climbed up the ladder and into the tunnel. He followed handholds and footholds up for about ten feet and came to another piece of plywood. He pushed on it, pushed again. It didn't budge. He closed his eyes. His head pounded.

He wedged his back against the wall and tried again, this time pushing with his feet. The plywood gave way, and the crisp smell of cool, fresh air filled his nostrils. He pushed the plywood aside with his feet and climbed out into the deepening dusk.

He had to get the others out. He couldn't just leave them. A rope. He'd seen one in the mining cart.

TWENTY-SEVEN

The police car had been parked outside the cabin for at least ten minutes, maybe fifteen, and Corey was getting anxious. What could they be talking about? She was crouched in the trees at the edge of the forest, hugging herself against the cold. The light jacket she wore wasn't designed for spending a night in the mountains.

She stood up, rubbing her arms. She couldn't wait much longer. She had to get to the road before Will's mother got here. But she was reluctant to cross the field. The moon had risen, and she would be easily spotted.

Then she saw a flashlight beam at the back of the cabin. Two men. Both tall. The sheriff and his son. She was less than fifty yards away from them, and the flashlight beam was moving away from the cabin. She took several steps back into the forest. Maybe they had forced Irene to talk. Or maybe they were looking for her tracks. She was glad now that she'd run along the well-trodden path toward the outhouse before she'd dashed to the trees.

Then the light disappeared. The trees blocked her view. Were they rushing toward her? Did they know she was here?

Panicking, she turned and ran further into the forest until she was gasping for air. She stopped, listened. After a few moments, she heard a car engine start up. They were leaving.

She raced to the edge of the field. The police car was nowhere in sight. She waited another thirty seconds, wondering if it was a trap. Then she bolted for the cabin and tapped on the back door.

"It's okay. They're gone," Irene said. "The sheriff said you were a runaway and had been seen near here. They kept questioning me, telling me that it was a crime to harbor a runaway, that your parents were worried and wanted you back home."

"My parents are out of town. I'm not a runaway."

Irene nodded. "Don't worry. I didn't believe him. He was too intense to be just chasing a runaway. I told him I hadn't seen anyone out here."

"So he believed you?"

"He backed off after I told him I used to be a police dispatcher in Colorado Springs and would never hide a runaway."

"Thanks. I better get out to the road."

Irene opened a drawer and handed Corey a flashlight. "Take this with you. You can signal her."

The minutes stretched on endlessly as Corey waited at the roadside. It seemed she'd been standing here for hours when she finally saw headlights moving her way. She clicked on the flashlight. What if it was the sheriff coming back? She hesitated as the vehicle appeared over a rise. She decided to take a chance. She waved the flashlight and a Grand Cherokee skidded to a stop next to her.

The window went down and a woman with light brown hair, who didn't look much like Will, leaned out. "Are you Corey?"

"That's right." She climbed inside. She could see that Will's mother was surprised she was black and probably wondered why Will had never mentioned her. But there was no time to get acquainted.

"I'm Marion Connors. Where's Will?"

Corey saw a gun in a holster resting on her lap. "About two miles down the road. Maybe less."

Corey tried to remember where the two vehicles had been blocking the road, but it was too dark now to pick out the spot. Then the car's high beams fell on the Land Rover they'd ridden in from town and a Ford Explorer, the vehicle Burke had driven.

Marion pulled off the road. She turned off the engine and unsnapped the holster on her gun.

As soon as Corey got out, she saw the glow of a cigarette and smelled burning tobacco. Burke ambled over to them. "Marion. What are you doing here?" His voice was low and threatening.

She raised her gun and aimed it at his head. "Where's Will? Tell me right now."

"C'mon, babe. Put that thing down. That's dangerous."

Marion cocked the gun. "Where is he, Tom? I'm not kidding."

"Okay, okay. He's in the mine. But it's going to blow up in about ten minutes. That's the truth, too."

For a moment, Corey thought Marion was going to shoot him. Then she turned to Corey. "Where—where is it?"

"This way." Corey flicked on the flashlight and ran along the darkened trail. Will's mother raced after her. If Burke was following, he was nowhere in sight.

It seemed longer this time, and she was beginning to worry that she'd missed the mine when the flashlight beam fell on the entrance to the tunnel. She hurried into it, Marion right behind her.

She moved past the mining cart and stopped at the door. She was surprised to see that the lock was still on the ground. Why hadn't Burke locked the door? Was it a trap?

"Hurry! Open it," Marion said. "Will, are you in there?" Corey put her hands on the door and was about to push when she heard voices yelling inside. She thought they were calling for help, but something made her hesitate. Something about the door.

"Go ahead. Open it!" Marion urged.

"No! Don't!" Will shouted from behind them. "Don't touch that door."

"Will!" Marion turned and ran to him.

"The door triggers a bomb!" Will yelled. "Get away from it."

Corey backed away, her heart pounding in her ears. Burke had wanted them to rush here and open the door. That was why he had been so quick to tell them where to find Will.

"How did you get out?" Marion asked, hugging Will.

"There's another way. We've got to help Dad and Grandpa and Detective Olsen." He pulled away from her, leaned over the mining cart, and snatched a rope. "We don't have much time."

TWENTY-EIGHT

Will dashed out of the tunnel, then scrambled up the steep hill. He slipped once, grabbed on to the trunk of an aspen sapling, and pulled himself to his feet.

Marion worked out at a gym and it showed. She was agile and kept within a few feet of him, and Corey was right behind her. The landscape leveled and Will was on his feet and running. He reached the hole he'd escaped from and dropped into it. He grabbed the lantern he'd left on the ground and threw the end of the rope to his mother. "Let it all out."

He found the footholds, clambered down to the ladder, and dropped onto the lab counter.

"Will, what are you doing?" Connors yelled. "This place is going to blow." He was now working on the thick rope binding Lansa's ankles. Olsen's feet were free, and she was leaning over the bomb looking at the timer.

"Listen to your grandfather," Olsen said. "There's nothing you can do for us."

"We can pull you out." He reached up for the rope to tie a loop for a harness, but realized it was too short.

Even if they were able to climb onto the counter, the rope wouldn't reach.

"It won't work," he said softly.

"Will, get out now!" Lansa shouted.

His head throbbed, his heart pounded. He held out the lantern and lowered himself to his hands and knees as he stared at the timer on the bomb. Two minutes left.

Will looked up at his father—to say good-bye to him, to apologize for failing him—but his view was blocked by a man in a long leather shirt, leggings, and boots. He wore two feathers in his long black hair. "Masau," Will whispered, recognizing the figure from his dreams.

The moment he said the name, the image shifted and Will was looking at Burke, who smiled and dropped down to one knee in front of the bomb. He reached down and put his fingers on a blue wire.

"Cut this one and it won't go off."

Will wasn't sure whether the voice was spoken aloud or was inside his head. He climbed down from the counter and looked at Connors. "Grandpa, give me your knife."

"Will!" Connors shouted. "Get out of here!"

"You don't have to die with us," Olsen said.

"Give it to him," Lansa said in an even voice. "He knows what he's doing."

His father knew. Somehow he knew what was going on. Connors tossed the pocketknife. Will picked it up, then dropped down on one knee in front of the bomb. He heard his mother calling him from above. His fingers were shaking. He looked at the clock. Fifty seconds left.

He reached for the wire. But now he saw there were two blue ones, one looping to the left, the other to the right. Which one was it?

He stared at the wires, sweat dripping from his brow, blurring his vision. He took the blue wire on the left between his finger tips. He hesitated, then pressed the knife to the wire. It sliced easily through the insulation, but the blade was dulled from cutting the rope. He sawed back and forth, pulling the wire over the blade.

C'mon. Cut.

He glanced at the timer. Fifteen seconds left. Ten. Nine. Eight.

The blade slit the wire.

He fell back and watched the seconds tick away. Four . . . three . . . two . . . one.

Nothing happened.

Just then he heard a muffled voice at the door. "Will, are you in there?"

The voice was familiar, but he couldn't place it. He saw the wire leading to the door. "Don't open that. . . ."

The door creaked open. Will tensed, still expecting an explosion. Again, nothing happened.

Then the bomb emitted a buzzing sound. His hands froze in the air; his breath caught in his throat. The sound stopped.

No one spoke. Will slowly stood up. His mother called his name again. "I think . . . I think we're safe," he replied.

"How did you do it?" Connors asked. "How did you know which wire to cut?"

"I had some help."

Coach Boorman and Aaron Thomas stood in the doorway, scanning the room. "My God," Boorman said. "Your mother called me from her car just as Aaron was telling me he thought you were set up."

Marion climbed down the ladder to the counter and turned to Boorman. "Did you call the state troopers?"

"You bet I did. They're on their way. Are you sure the sheriff is involved?"

"I'm more than sure," Olsen said from the other side of the room.

Will touched the back pocket of his jeans and was relieved to find that Burke's notebook was still there. "I've got proof, too."

"Oh, no!" Marion said in a low voice.

Will followed her gaze past Boorman. Burke was standing behind Boorman, his snub-nosed .38 in his hand. He was staring at the bomb. His eyes looked glazed.

No one moved.

But Burke simply turned and walked away without saying a word. A moment later, a single shot rang out, echoing through the lab.

EPILOGUE

The wind swept through the ghost town of Ashcroft warning of the approach of winter. Will and Corey were both bundled in parkas as they walked down the main street of the deserted, crumbling town. Will peered into the open doorways of the sagging buildings as if he expected to see Myra's ghost.

"You miss her, don't you?" Corey asked.

Will nodded. "I needed to come here one more time. It's the last place we were together," he said as if she didn't already know.

He stopped in front of a doorway, the same one he and Myra had entered the night of her death. They walked into the building. The bare wood walls and beams looked skeletal in the light of midday.

"She wanted to tell me something when we came here that night. Now I know it was about the drug and the factory. She'd found out, but was too frightened to say anything."

"Why didn't she tell you?"

"I didn't give her a chance."

He moved over to the window and to his amazement saw the red fox he'd seen when he was here with Myra. His ears were poised, his brown eyes staring at him from the high grass. He pointed it out to Corey.

"I saw him that night, too."

"Even though she didn't have a chance to tell you, you still found out. She left you with a challenge, and you succeeded."

It was not only a challenge, he thought, it became part of Hawk Moon, his initiation into the Hopi tribe. "I couldn't have figured it out without your help."

She looked up at him and smiled. "You helped me, too. I came out of my shell. I think I can accept this place now." She laughed. "I'm accepting Aspen and you're leaving."

"How did you know?"

"I didn't. I just had a feeling that you're going to live with your dad."

"You're right. I'm going to finish high school on the reservation. I'm starting after the holidays."

She nodded. "I hope it works out for you."

"Me too." He reached into his jacket pocket and took out a small package. "This is for you. Call it an early Christmas present."

Corey gazed at the package, which fit into her palm, then she carefully removed the wrappings. Inside was a small box. She opened it. "Oh, Will. It's beautiful."

She held up the miniature kachina with a cylindrical mask that was red and blue and yellow with red buttonlike eyes and mouth. Feathers protruded from the top. A tiny shawl was draped over its shoulders and it wore a brown kilt.

"It's Masau. He's a guardian and a trickster, too. Sort of like the fox."

"Thanks, Will." She raised her head and smiled.

He looked out the window again. The fox was gone.